P9-EDP-421

GEORGIA BOY

ERSKINE CALDWELL

GEORGIA
BOY

Foreword by Roy Blount Jr.

Brown Thrasher Books

THE UNIVERSITY OF GEORGIA PRESS

ATHENS AND LONDON

Riverside Community College
Library
4800 Magnolia Avenue
Riverside, California 92506

MAY   '97

PS 3505 .A322 G4 1995

Caldwell, Erskine, 1903–

Georgia boy

Published in 1995 as a Brown Thrasher Book
by the University of Georgia Press, Athens, Georgia 30602
© 1943, 1971 by Erskine Caldwell
Foreword to the Brown Thrasher Edition © 1995
by the University of Georgia Press
All rights reserved

The paper in this book meets the guidelines for
permanence and durability of the Committee on
Production Guidelines for Book Longevity of the
Council on Library Resources.

Printed in the United States of America

96 97 98 99 P 5 4 3 2

Library of Congress Cataloging in Publication Data

Caldwell, Erskine, 1903 –
Georgia boy / Erskine Caldwell; foreword by Roy Blount Jr.
p.   cm.
"Brown thrasher books."
ISBN 0-8203-1736-5 (pbk. : alk. paper)
1. Georgia—Social life and customs—Fiction.
2. Country life—Georgia—Fiction.   I. Title.
PS3505.A322G4   1995
813'.52—dc20   95-13815

British Library Cataloging in Publication Data available

For JUNE *with love*

CONTENTS

FOREWORD

Roy Blount Jr.

Tobacco Road and *God's Little Acre* are vivid, heaven knows. They're the inverse of over-the-top: under-the-bottom. Once they get into your mind's basement you can't root them out. But they sure don't make me want to get up on the roof and dance. Ain't *anybody* going to be able to do anything with those people; those people ain't *ever* going to have anything nice.

Now deeply trashy doings have been the glory of southern humor. George Washington Harris's Sut Lovingood is incorrigibly rank; Joel Chandler Harris's bestiary of brers treat each other scandalously; Mark Twain's rogues deserve to be tarred and feathered. But comedy calls for a shaft of exhilaration.

You have to give Jeeter and Ty Ty and them credit for how indefatigably they self-defeat, but they actually seem to be loading the deck against themselves. They're based on a po' white family that Erskine Caldwell's minister father tried and failed to take under his wing, and I can't help thinking that the author is getting back at them for

ix

being too much for his daddy. When Jeeter is eating that bag of turnips, hey, that is pretty wonderful in its way, but *Tobacco Road* and *God's Little Acre* make it too easy for the reader to regard all these people askance.

Georgia Boy is something else again, ethnically and Oedipally. To my mind this gracefully braided volume of rough-cut stories amounts to Caldwell's most satisfying novel. Until recently I had never read all the stories in sequence. When I did, I felt them shifting, modulating, and building up to an end that reverberates all the way back through to the start.

Reviewers have tended to describe these stories as light and fondly nostalgic, but that must be only in comparison with *Tobacco Road* and *God's Little Acre*. The truth is I didn't feel right about actually laughing until page 205. I take it back: I laughed two or three times during "My Old Man and the Grass Widow," especially when Ma bites Mrs. Weatherbee, the teenage widow woman, on the bare foot.

But the widow story is the most benign one. Handsome Brown, the "Negro yardboy" who is treated like an all-purpose appliance, does not appear in the widow story, so we don't have to watch him be compelled to do something horrible: to plunge from a roof full of goats straight into a well, or to hang onto a tree all night while woodpeckers peck his head. And in the widow story Ma comes out sufficiently on top (might it be, even, that the feather at the end is for her?) that spousal neglect seems more or less avenged.

That story aside, however, I could not see my way clear to laughing until the aforementioned page 205, the last line of "The Night My Old Man Came Home." That line made me give up and chortle with both immediate and retrospective delight. And it set me up suspensefully for what was coming.

I hate a foreword that is too forthcoming, so I won't give that line away here. And I urge you not to skip ahead to it. I'm trying to share my reading with you, but that won't work if you cheat.

And let me say that this is a really sticky book for a white man to write an appreciation of. Sexist and racist don't even touch the attitudes and practices of Morris Stroup, the Georgia-boy narrator's beloved, incorrigible father. By any civilized standard Morris is an execrable family man, employer, and citizen. He is lazy, harebrained, and out for himself. He will lie and he will steal, he will disappear for long periods, he will come home furniture-smashing drunk, and he will fool around. And he will for all intents and purposes keep a black person enslaved.

The old man not only will do all those things but also will do them just naturally, over and over, without ever

xi

considering that he shouldn't. Part of me hates to say so (I believe you will be able to guess which part I mean), but it is justice, not only poetic but also intergendered, when Ma takes the drastic measure she takes at the end of the last story, "My Old Man Hasn't Been the Same Since."

It is good that the book ends that way. But Morris is an enduringly fresh character. You can see why his boy is so fond of him, even when the old man appropriates the money the boy was saving for the Wild West show and blows it on checking out the girlie show and bouncing baseballs off the wretchedly resilient head of Handsome Brown. Morris Stroup is a better show than the Wild West one could have been. He is the real thing, a wild Georgia cracker. *Georgia Boy's* other characters are real, too.

If either Ma or Handsome or William, the boy, were ones to take fully deserved pity on themselves, the whole affair would be spoiled. But these people are fatalistic, and as spirited as possible, which is considerably. They are not exactly soft-hearted—they can't afford to be too sensitive. They are long-suffering—up to a point—because they have to be. If they had Morris's opportunities they might act the same way. Maleness is Morris's only privilege, and by his lights he (unlike Huck's Pap) makes the most of it. I have to figure that Morris and William

xii

get a message at the end, though. The father won't ever be the same, and the son won't be what his father was.

Caldwell wrote several of these stories in Russia, where he had gone with the woman to whom he was then married, the noted and strong-willed photographer Margaret Bourke-White. She was doing what she wanted to there, and he was moping.

The story he wrote first, by his account (according to his recent biographer, he wrote it before going to Russia), was "The Night My Old Man Came Home," the one whose last line made me laugh so hard. You can see these stories as male wish-fulfillment, as a free spirit's resistance of female domination (the only part I can't quite buy is Morris's outslicking the gypsy woman); but they're too calmly, unsentimentally harsh to be that simple.

Politically as well as literarily, this is no *Huckleberry Finn*. But that may be in part because *Georgia Boy* is tougher. These stories don't even obliquely protest the lot of—to take the most oppressed and affable character— Handsome Brown. But they do portray that lot unblinkingly and—though this is a close call—uncondescendingly. When it comes to hanging on to what he can, Handsome is as staunch as conditions allow. (You might want to look up two other Caldwell stories, "The Negro in the Well" and "The End of Christy Tucker,"

xiii

which similarly if more grimly transcend interracial "compassion," and which convey how little room black people had to protest, themselves, in that time and place.)

The young boy's stories do celebrate, against the grain of the golden rule, the improbably flexible lot of an old boy who has come up poor, hard, and trashy, and preserving a spark.

The spark is real and what's so funny.

I

MY OLD MAN'S BALING MACHINE

I

MY OLD MAN'S BALING MACHINE

THERE was a big commotion in front of the house, sounding as though somebody had dumped a load of rocks on our steps. The building shook a little on its foundations, and then everything was quiet. Ma and I were on the back porch when we heard the noise, and we didn't know what to make of it. Ma said she was afraid it was the crack of doom, and she told me to hurry and turn the wringer handle faster so she could get Mrs. Dudley's laundry wrung and pinned on the clothesline before something terrible happened.

"I want to go see what it was, Ma," I said, turning the wringer handle with all my might. "Can't I, Ma? Can't I go see what it was?"

"You turn that handle, William," she said, shaking her head and feeding a pair of Mr. Dudley's overalls into the wringer. "Whatever it was can wait until I get this laundry hung on the line."

I cranked the wringer as fast as I could, listening at

the same time. I heard somebody talking in a loud voice in front of the house, but I could not make out anything that was said.

Just then my old man came running around the corner.

"What on earth's the matter, Morris?" Ma asked.

"Where's Handsome?" my old man said, short of breath. "Where's Handsome at?"

Handsome Brown was our Negro yardboy who had worked for us ever since I could remember.

"Handsome's cleaning up in the kitchen, like he should be," Ma said. "What do you want with him?"

"I need him right away to give me a lift," Pa said. "I need Handsome in a big hurry."

"I'll help, Pa," I said, backing away from the wringer. "Let me help, Pa."

"William," Ma said, catching me by the arm and pulling me back, "you turn that wringer handle like I told you."

Just then Handsome stuck his head out the kitchen door. My old man saw him right away.

"Handsome," Pa said, "drop everything and come around to the front of the house. I need you to give me a lift right away."

4

Handsome looked at Ma before he made a move, waiting to hear what she had to say about his leaving the kitchen work. Ma didn't say anything then, because she was busy feeding one of Mrs. Dudley's faded old calico mother-hubbards into the wringer. My old man grabbed Handsome by the sleeve and pulled him down the steps and across the yard. They were out of sight around the house in another minute.

I wanted to go with them, but every time I looked up at Ma I knew better than to ask again. I turned the wringer with all my might, trying to get the wringing finished as soon as possible.

It wasn't long until we heard the front door open, and soon afterward there was a heavy thud in the hall. It sounded exactly as though the roof had caved in.

Ma and I both ran inside to find out what had happened. When we reached the hall, my old man and Handsome were tugging and pulling at a heavy big box that was painted bright red like a freight car and had a big iron wheel on top. The box was as big as an old-fashioned melodeon and just as curious-looking. Handsome gave it a mighty shove, and the whole thing went through the door and came down on the parlor floor so heavily that it shook the pictures hanging on the walls. Ma and I squeezed through the door at the same time. My old man was standing there beside the big red box, patting it with his hand and panting like a dog that had been running rabbits all morning.

"What on earth, Morris?" Ma said, walking around the box and trying to figure out what it was.

"Ain't it a beauty, Martha?" he said, panting between each word. He sat down in a rocking chair and looked at the box admiringly. "Ain't it a beauty, though?"

"Where did it come from, Pa?" I asked him, but he was so busy looking at it he did not hear me.

Handsome walked around it, peeping through the cracks to see if he could see anything inside.

"Did somebody give it to you, Morris?" Ma asked, standing back and doing her best to size it up. "Where in the world did you get it?"

"I bought it," Pa said. "I just a little while ago made the deal. The fellow who makes a habit of selling them came through town this morning and I bought one off him."

"What did you pay for it?" Ma asked, concerned.

"Fifty cents down, and fifty cents a week," Pa said.

"For how many weeks?" Ma asked.

"For all the weeks in a year," he said. "That ain't much. Shucks, when you come to think about it, it's hardly nothing to speak of. The year'll go by in no time. It won't be a strain at all."

"What's it for?" Ma said. "What does it do?"

"It's a baling machine," he said. "It bales paper. You put in a lot of old paper, like old wornout newspapers, and such, and then you wind the wheel down tight on top, and it comes out at the bottom in a hard bale, all tied with wire. It's a mighty invention."

"What is you going to do with it after it comes out at the bottom, Mr. Morris?" Handsome asked.

"Sell it, of course," Pa said. "The fellow comes around once a week and buys up all the paper I've baled. He takes out his fifty cents, and hands me the balance due me."

"Well, I declare," Handsome said. "It sure is a fine thing, all right."

"Where are you going to get all the paper to put into the machine?" Ma asked.

"Shucks," my old man said, "that's the easiest part of it all. Old paper is always lying around everywhere. Things like old wornout newspapers, and such. Even the wrapping paper from the stores goes right into it.

7

When the wind blows a piece of paper down the street, that goes into it, too. It's a money-making machine if there ever was one."

Ma went up closer and looked down inside. Then she gave the wheel on top a whirl and walked to the door.

"The parlor's no place for it," she said. "Take that contraption out of my best room, Morris Stroup."

Pa ran after her.

"But Martha, there ain't no better place fit for it. You wouldn't have me set it out in the weather to rust and rot, would you? It's a valuable machine."

"You take it out, or I'll have Handsome chop it up for stovewood," she said, going down the hall and out to the back porch.

My old man came back and looked at the baling machine, running his hands over the smooth wooden sides. He didn't say anything, but after a minute he reached down and got a grip on it and lifted. Handsome and I got at the other end and lifted it up. We carried it through the parlor door and out to the front porch. Pa set down his end, and we dropped ours.

"This'll do," Pa said. "It'll be out of the sun and rain here on the porch."

8

He began unwinding the big wheel on top.

"Handsome," he said, "you go get me all the old paper you can lay your hands on. We're going to start in right away."

Handsome and I went through the house, gathering up all the paper we could find. There was a stack of old newspapers in one of the closets, and I carried those out and Pa dumped them into the hopper. Handsome came back with a big armful of wrapping paper he had found somewhere. My old man took it and stuffed it down into the machine.

"We'll have a hundred-pound bale in no time at all," Pa said. "Then after that first one, everything else will be pure profit. We'll have more money than we'll know what to do with. It might be a good idea to buy three or four more of the machines off the fellow when he comes back to Sycamore next week, because we can bale paper faster than one machine can handle it. We'll have so much money in no time at all that I'll have to trust some of it to the bank. It's a shame I didn't know about this way of making money before, because it's the easiest way I ever heard of. I'll bale me so much paper at this rate that it won't be no time at all before I can quit and retire."

9

He stopped and shoved Handsome towards the door.

"Handsome, get a hustle on and bring out more of that old waste paper."

Handsome went inside and began looking through the dresser drawers and in the closets and behind the wash-stand. I found some old magazines on the parlor table and took them out to Pa.

"That's right, son," he said. "Old magazines are just as worthless as old newspapers and they weigh a heap more. Go get all the magazines you can find."

By the time I got back with another load my old man said we had enough for a second bale. We got to work and pressed it down tight and Handsome tied it with baling wire. Pa dumped it on the floor and told Handsome to stack it up on top of the first bale.

We worked away for another hour, and it wasn't long until we had three bales stacked up in the corner of the porch. Handsome told us he couldn't find any more paper anywhere in the whole house, and my old man said he would go look himself. He was gone a long time, but when he came back he had a big armful of song books that Ma had ordered for her Sunday School class. We tore the backs off them, because the backs were covered with cloth, and my old man said it wouldn't be honest to try to pass off cloth for paper. After that he went back inside for a while and came out with an armful of letters tied up with ribbons. He tore off the ribbons and dumped them into the hopper. When everything had been baled, it was close to noon, and Pa said we could knock off for an hour.

We started in again right after dinner. We looked all over the house several times, but couldn't find anything more made of paper, except some loose wallpaper in one of the rooms, which Pa said ought to come down anyway, because it was so old and shabby-looking on the walls. After that he sent Handsome and me down the street to Mrs. Price's house to ask her if she had any old paper she had no more use for. We made two trips to Mrs. Price's. By then all of us were tired out, and Pa said he thought we had done enough work for the day. We all sat down on the front steps and counted the number of bales stacked in the corner. There were seven of them. Pa said that was a good start, and that if we did as well every day, we would soon be as rich as anybody in town.

We sat there a long time thinking about all the paper we had baled, and my old man said we'd all get up early the next morning and that maybe by night we'd be able to count twelve bales instead of seven for the day's work. Ma came out in a little while and looked at the big stack of baled paper. My old man turned around and waited for her to say how pleased she was that we had done so much work the first day.

"Where did all this paper come from, Morris?" she asked, walking over to the bales and pulling at them.

"From all over the place, Martha," Pa said. "We got rid of all the old paper lying around the place that was just getting in the way. We found a lot of it stuffed away in places that would have been rat nests before long. It's a good thing I happened to get hold of this machine. The cleaning up has made the house look better already."

Ma poked her finger into one of the bales and pulled out something. It was one of the magazines.

"What's this, Morris?" she said, looking around.

She pulled out another magazine.

"Do you know what you've gone and done, Morris Stroup!" she said. "You've taken all my recipes and dress patterns I've been saving ever since I started housekeeping with you!"

"But it's all so old it's not worth anything," Pa said.

12

Handsome started backing through the hall door. Ma looked around.

"Handsome, untie every one of those bales," she said. "I want to see what else you've gone and taken of mine. Do like I tell you, Handsome!"

"But, Martha—" Pa said.

"Ma, can't we sell the old newspapers and magazines?" I asked.

"Shut up, William," she said. "Stop taking up for your Pa."

Handsome pulled the wire loose, and stacks of song books and magazines began tumbling to the floor. Ma stooped down and picked up one of the books.

"My heavens above!" Ma cried. "These are the new song books for my Sunday School class that we took up the collection for. Those poor trusting souls thought their song books would be safe in my house. And now just look at them!"

She began digging into the pile of papers and magazines on the floor. Then she began digging into one of the other bales. She jerked off the wire before Handsome had a chance to break it.

"What's this, Morris?" she said, raising her voice

13

and staring at one of the letters we had brought out and baled.

"It's just a piece of old waste paper I found stuffed away in a closet," Pa said. "The rats and mice would have chewed them up sooner or later, anyway."

Ma's face became red all over, and she sat down heavily in a chair. She did not say anything for a minute. Then she called Handsome.

"Handsome," she said, biting her lips a little and dabbing at her eyes with her apron, "undo that bale this minute!"

Handsome leaped across the pile of paper on the floor and pulled the baling wire loose. The whole pile of letters fell in a heap on the floor at Ma's feet. She reached down and picked up a handful. When she read some of the writing in one of the letters, she screamed.

"What's the matter, Martha?" Pa asked her, getting up and crossing the porch to where she was.

"My letters!" Ma said, dabbing at her eyes with her apron. "All the love and courtship letters I've been saving from my old beaus! All the letters you ever wrote me, Morris! Now, just look at what you've gone and done!"

14

"But they ain't nothing but old letters, Martha," Pa said. "I could write you some new ones almost any time, if you want me to."

"I don't want new ones," she said; "I want to keep the old ones!"

She burst out crying so loud Pa did not know what to do. He walked to the other end of the porch and came back.

Ma reached down and picked up as many letters as she could hold in her apron.

"I'll write you some new letters, Martha," Pa said.

Ma got up.

"It looks like you'd have more respect for the letters all my other beaus wrote me," she said, "even if you didn't have any for the ones you wrote me."

She lifted the apronful of letters and went inside, slamming the door behind her.

My old man walked up and down through the litter of loose papers and song books, kicking through them with his feet. He did not say anything for a while, but after that he walked back to the baling machine and rubbed his hands over the smooth wooden sides.

"It seems like a shame to see all this paper go to

waste, son," he said. "It's a pity your Ma had to go and take on so about old letters and things. We could have made us a heap of money selling them to the fellow when he comes to town again next week."

II

*THE DAY WE RANG THE BELL FOR
PREACHER HAWSHAW*

II

THE DAY WE RANG THE BELL FOR
PREACHER HAWSHAW

WHEN I got home from school, Preacher Hawshaw, the Universalist minister, was standing
on our front porch talking to my old man. I didn't pay
much attention to them at first, because Preacher Hawshaw was always coming to our house and trying to
make my old man promise to go to church on Sunday,
but Pa always had a good excuse for not going, usually
saying Ida, our sugar mule, had the colic and that he
couldn't afford to leave her all alone until she got well,
or that Mr. Jess Johnson's hogs were running wild and
that he had to stay at home to keep them from rooting up our garden, and so I thought they were arguing
about the same thing as they always did. I stopped at
the bottom of the steps to listen to them, wondering
what excuse Pa was going to use that time, and the first
thing I heard was Preacher Hawshaw saying that old
Uncle Jeff Davis Fletcher, the colored janitor of the

Universalist church, had gone over into the next county to visit some sick relations for a few days and that there was nobody to ring the church bell that afternoon during Miss Susie Thing's wedding when she was going to marry Hubert Willy, the substitute mail carrier. My old man listened to all Preacher Hawshaw had to say, but he didn't show any signs of wanting to ring the bell for him.

"I tell you what, Mr. Stroup," Preacher Hawshaw said, after waiting a long time for my old man to say something. "If you'll ring the bell while the wedding's taking place this afternoon, I won't pester you about attending church services the whole rest of the year. Now, ain't that fair, Mr. Stroup?"

"It would be a heap more fairer if you'd promise never to pester me about going to church—this year or any year to come," Pa told him.

"That's asking a great deal of me, Mr. Stroup," he said slowly. "It's my duty to keep after folks until they go to church."

"If you want the bell rung bad enough," my old man said, "you'll treat me like a Methodist or Baptist, and stop trying to make me go to the Universalist church to hear you preach. I've got a religion of my own, and if it's good enough for me, listening to a Universalist preacher preach would only make me dissatisfied with what I've got. You wouldn't want to be the cause of making me turn my back on my own religion, would you?"

Preacher Hawshaw leaned against the wall as if he were all tired out, and thought for a long time. Pa sat where he was on the banister and waited for him to make up his mind.

"Let's not discuss religion any more today, Mr. Stroup," he said at last. "I'm all fagged out, and I've got that marriage ceremony to perform in less than half an hour. It's too late for me to hunt up anybody else to ring the bell, and if you don't ring it for me, I'll be in a pretty pickle."

My old man got up from the banister and walked down the steps into the yard. Preacher Hawshaw followed him as fast as he could.

"I'll ring it for you this time, just to help you out," Pa said. "Nobody has ever been able to accuse me of refusing to lend a helping hand in a time of trouble."

"That's fine!" Preacher Hawshaw said, smiling and beaming at Pa. "I knew all along I could count on you, Mr. Stroup!"

He began dusting off his clothes and adjusting his necktie.

"Now, there's not much to do," he said. "All you have to remember is to ring the bell the instant I start reading the marriage ceremony, and keep on ringing it until the bride and groom have left the church and passed out of sight down the street. When you can't see hide or hair of them any longer, you'll know it's time to quit ringing it. That's plain enough, now ain't it, Mr. Stroup?"

"I couldn't get balled up doing a simple thing like that," my old man told him. "It'll be as easy as falling off a log."

He backed down the path towards the street.

"I've got to hurry over to the church now," he said nervously. "The ceremony is due to start in about twenty minutes. You dress yourself up and come over there as fast as you can, Mr. Stroup. I'll be waiting in the vestibule right beside the bell-rope."

Preacher Hawshaw turned around and hurried off towards the Universalist church three blocks away. My old man started inside the house.

"Come on, son," he said to me, waving his arm in

a big sweep. "Let's get ready to go to the wedding. I'll need you to help me ring that bell. Come on!"

We went inside and Pa doused his head in the wash basin and slicked down his hair with the brush. As soon as he had finished that, we were ready to go.

"Will you let me ring it some by myself, Pa?" I asked, running along beside him in order to keep up. "Can I, Pa?"

"We'll see when we get there, son," he told me. "If it ain't too heavy for you to pull all by yourself, you can."

People were walking towards the church already, and we passed them and hurried ahead so we would be there in plenty of time to start ringing the bell. There was a crowd of people standing in front of the church when we got there, but Pa only waved at them and we hurried into the vestibule.

Preacher Hawshaw was standing right beside the bell-rope just as he said he would be doing. He was pretty nervous by that time, and it was all he could do to keep still in one place. As soon as he saw us, he began pacing up and down and glancing at his watch every few steps.

"This is an important wedding, Mr. Stroup," he

23

whispered out loud to Pa. "The parties represent two of the firm pillars of my church. I wouldn't want anything to go wrong for the whole world. This marriage means a lot to me. It will unite two bickering families and heal the bad blood that's been keeping the whole congregation upset."

"You don't have to worry over my part," Pa told him. "You just go ahead about the rest of your business, and I'll take care of the bell-ringing. I used to ring the bell at the school house when I was the janitor up there, and I know all there is to know about ringing bells."

"I'm glad to hear that, Mr. Stroup," he said, wiping his face with his handkerchief. "It's a big load off my mind to be able to turn the bell-ringing over to an experienced hand."

The people were walking into the church by that time, and the organist began playing music. Pretty soon I saw Miss Susie Thing, all dressed up in fluffy white clothes and carrying a big armful of flowers, come in one of the side doors. Almost at the same time Hubert Willy came in one of the other doors. That was a sign that the wedding was about to begin and I told my old man that it looked as if it would be time to start ring-

ing the bell almost any minute. Preacher Hawshaw
came running back up the aisle, looking at his watch
and almost tripping over somebody's foot that was
sticking out from one of the benches.

"All right, Mr. Stroup!" he whispered in a hoarse
loud voice to Pa. "As soon as you see me reach down
and pick up my little black book from the table, you'll
know it's time for you to start ringing the bell."

Pa nodded and got a good grip on the heavy thick
rope that hung down from the belfry through a large
round hole in the ceiling.

"Grab a good hold on it, son," he told me. "It'll take
both of us to get this thing started. It's a heap bigger
than the school-house bell."

Both of us got good grips on the rope as high up as
we could reach.

"Now," Pa told me, "look at Preacher Hawshaw and
tell me when it's time to pull on this rope."

Miss Susie Thing and Hubert Willy walked up in
front of Preacher Hawshaw. Hubert's face was as red
as a beet, but I couldn't see Miss Susie's because she
had her face almost buried in the big bunch of flowers.
Preacher Hawshaw reached down and picked up the
little black book he had told us about.

"Now's the time, Pa!" I whispered as loud as I dared. "They're starting off!"

We pulled on the heavy rope until we got the bell swinging back and forth in the belfry. Pa showed me how to pull down as hard as I could, and then to turn loose and let the rope run back upward through the hole in the ceiling. After five or six times the clapper hit the bell, and we had the rope going up and down the way we wanted it.

The bell was ringing long beats that sounded a little peculiar, but I looked up into my old man's face and he looked so pleased that I decided it was ringing the way it should. I happened to look down the aisle just then, though, and I saw Preacher Hawshaw beckon to an usher and whisper something to him. A lot of people were turning around in their seats and looking back towards us in the vestibule as though we were doing something wrong. The usher came running up the aisle, and as soon as he got to us, he leaned forward and whispered in Pa's ear.

My old man shook his head and went on ringing the bell just as we had done from the start. The usher hurried back to where Preacher Hawshaw was standing in front of Miss Susie and Hubert. Preacher Hawshaw

26

had already stopped reading from the little black book, and as soon as the usher whispered something to him, he laid the book on the table and came running up the aisle towards us.

"Look here, Mr. Stroup!" he said out loud. "Quit tolling that bell!"

"What are you talking about?" Pa asked him. We kept on pulling the bell-rope and letting it run back upwards through the hole in the ceiling just as we had from the start. "I'm ringing the bell like you told me. What's wrong?"

"What's wrong!" Preacher Hawshaw said, running his finger around the inside of his collar to loosen it up. Don't you hear that *ding-dong, ding-dong* up there in the belfry?" Everybody in the church had turned around by that time and a lot of them were making motions at us with their hands. "What you're doing is tolling the bell. That's for a funeral. Stop making it *ding-dong!*"

"What in the world do you want me to do?" my old man asked him. "When I was the janitor at the school house, I rang it just like I'm doing now. Nobody ever accused me of tolling it then."

"The school-house bell ain't nothing compared in

27

size to this one, Mr. Stroup," Preacher Hawshaw said. "There's all the difference in the world in size. The school-house bell would make the same sound no matter how you rang it. Now, quit ringing this bell the way you're doing. It makes people sad. It don't set the right mood for a wedding."

"What do you want me to do to it, then?" Pa asked.

"Trill it!"

"Trill it?" my old man said. "What's that?"

Preacher Hawshaw turned and took a quick look at the people in the church. Miss Susie and Hubert were still standing down in front of the pulpit waiting for Preacher Hawshaw to come back and finish reading the wedding ceremony, but Miss Susie looked as if she might drop out of sight any second, and Hubert looked as though he might leap right through the stained-glass window.

"Ain't you ever trilled a bell in your life?" Preacher Hawshaw asked.

"More than that," Pa told him, "I ain't never heard about it before."

"It goes *ding-a-ling, ding-a-ling-ding,*" he said.

"It does?" Pa asked, still pulling on the rope the way

we had from the beginning. "That's something I never knew about, neither."

"Well, stop tolling it and begin trilling it, Mr. Stroup!" Preacher Hawshaw said. "There're people in there who've already begun to cry!"

"I just can't change over right here in the middle of things," Pa told him. "I'll need practice, anyway. I'll just have to keep on like I'm doing. Next time I'll do it the other way for you."

Preacher Hawshaw reached out to pull the rope himself, but just then Miss Susie Thing's brother, Jule, rushed up to Hubert Willy and shoved him out through the side door into the cemetery, accusing Hubert of having something to do with the way the bell was ringing. Before anybody could get out there, Jule had begun fighting Hubert, and in another minute they were fist-fighting all over the graves and tombstones. Hubert's nose began to bleed, and Jule tore a big hole in his pants when he stumbled over a wrought-iron marker on one of the graves that said, "Keep Off."

My old man told me to keep on ringing the bell while he went outside to watch the fist-fight. Preacher Hawshaw went, too, like everybody else in the church. I kept on ringing the bell just as we had from the start, and by then I could tell that it did make a *ding-dong* sound exactly like old Uncle Jeff Davis Fletcher rang it for funerals. Both Jule and Hubert were pretty badly beaten up by that time, but nobody tried to stop them, because everyone figured that the best thing to do was to let them fight it out and stop of their own accord when they were too tired to keep it up any longer. I pulled on the rope just like my old man told me to do, wondering how the same bell could make a *ding-a-ling, ding-a-ling-ding* sound as well as the *ding-dong* one, and right then Preacher Hawshaw came running in and jerked the rope out of my hands. The bell-clapper struck a couple of more times and then stopped.

"That's enough, William!" he said, grabbing me by the shirt and flinging me out of the vestibule and down the front steps.

Just then my old man came running around the corner of the church. He missed hearing the bell ring, and he stopped dead in his tracks.

"What did you quit for, son?" he asked me.

"Preacher Hawshaw told me to," I said. "He pushed me outside."

"He did!" my old man said, getting mad.

Preacher Hawshaw came out through the door and stopped on the top step. He looked all tired out.

"Now, look here, preacher!" Pa began. "When I agreed to ring the bell, I made up my mind to ring it or else to bust my buttons off in the effort. I'm going back inside there and finish the job like I promised to do. If you don't like the way I ring it, that ain't no fault of mine."

"Oh no, you don't!" Preacher Hawshaw said, blocking the door. "You've already broken up a wedding and caused a disgraceful fist-fight in the cemetery. The Things and the Willys have had their old sores opened up just because you tolled that bell. I don't want you to ever touch that bell-rope again."

"How in the world was I to know you wanted it rung *ding-a-ling, ding-a-ling-ding* instead of *ding-dong, ding-dong?*"

"Common sense ought to have told you that," he said, shoving my old man away from the door. "Besides, a man who doesn't know the difference between tolling a bell and trilling it hasn't got any business touching a church bell."

The people who had come to the church to see the wedding began talking about the way my old man had made the feud between the Things and the Willys come back. Miss Susie, who had been crying all that time in the choir loft, ran down the street toward her house still holding the big bouquet of flowers. I didn't see Jule and Hubert again, but I supposed they had gone home to wash up.

"You mean you just naturally don't like the way I rang the bell for you?" my old man asked Preacher Hawshaw.

"That's exactly right, Mr. Stroup," he said, giving Pa a big shove away from the door and making him hop down the steps in order to keep his footing.

"Then don't never come to my house again begging me to come to church to hear you preach," Pa said, turning and walking sidewise toward the street. "If you don't like my bell-ringing, I sure wouldn't take to your preaching."

Preacher Hawshaw went inside the vestibule. He was almost out of sight when my old man called him.

"What am I going to do about getting recognized religion if I take a notion that I need it?" Pa asked him. "I might decide recognized religion's something I ought to have, instead of my own private kind, and I don't want to be left high and dry when everybody else's being saved and sent to Heaven."

Preacher Hawshaw stuck his head out the door.

"You'll be better off among the Methodists or Baptists," he said. "The Universalists can get along without you, Mr. Stroup."

III

HANDSOME BROWN AND THE AGGRAVATING GOATS

III

HANDSOME BROWN AND THE AGGRAVATING GOATS

"IF it's not one thing your Pa's done," Ma said, looking all helpless and worn, "it's something else. I declare, sometimes I think I'll never have a minute's peace as long as I live."

She walked up and down in the backyard wringing her hands, trying to think of something to do.

The goats that Pa and Handsome Brown had brought home from our farm in the country were standing on top of the house chewing and looking down at us. The big billy goat had long white chin whiskers that made him look exactly like Mr. Carter who lived across the street.

"What in the world am I going to do?" Ma said, still walking up and down. "I've invited the Ladies' Social Circle to meet here this afternoon, and if those goats are still up on top of the house when they get here, I'll simply die of mortification."

37

The two nanny goats were chewing, too, but their whiskers were not nearly as long as the big goat's. In addition to the three grown goats up on the rooftop, there were two little kids up there. The kids were only two months old and they were only a quarter of the size of the billy, but all five of them up there together on top of the house looked like a lot of goats.

"William, tell Handsome to go downtown and find your Pa and tell him to come home and get those goats down right away," she said to me.

Handsome was cleaning up in the kitchen, and all I had to do was go to the edge of the porch and call him. He came out and asked me what we wanted.

"The first thing I want you to do, Handsome Brown," Ma said angrily, "is to tell me what on earth you meant by bringing those goats here."

"I only done what Mr. Morris told me to do, like I always does when you or Mr. Morris tells me to do something, Mis' Martha," he said, shifting from one foot to the other. "Mr. Morris said he wanted them goats brung home and he told me to drive them, and I done just that. You oughtn't blame me too much for what Mr. Morris told me to do, Mis' Martha."

"Why didn't you tell Mr. Morris he ought to ask

me first, then?" she said. "You thought of that, didn't you?"

"Yes, ma'm, I thought of it, but when I got ready to mention it to Mr. Morris, Mr. Morris said, 'The devil you say,' just like that, and that's why I ended up driving them here like I done."

Ma got madder than ever. She picked up a piece of stove wood and slung it at the goats on top of the house, but the stick fell halfway short of reaching them. It slammed against the side of the house, making a big noise and leaving a mark on the weatherboarding.

"Go downtown this instant and find Mr. Morris," she told Handsome, "and tell him I want to see him right away. Look in the barber shop and the hardware store and every place he loafs until you find him. And don't you dare come back without him, Handsome Brown. I don't want to hear any excuses from you this time."

"Yes, ma'm, Mis' Martha," Handsome said, trotting off to look for Pa.

The goats walked along the ridge plate on the roof, looking down into the backyard at Ma and me part of the time, and the rest of the time looking down the other side into the street. They had got up there by

39

hopping from the woodpile to the woodshed, from there to the porch roof, then leaping up on top of the kitchen roof, and from there to the main part of the house. They were about two stories and a half high above us on the ground, and it was a funny sight to see the three large goats and the two little kids walking Indian file across the top of the roof.

The next time they stopped and looked down at us, the billy chewed some more, making his whiskers sway, and it looked exactly as though he were making faces at us.

Ma tried to find another stick of wood to throw at him, but she was too mad then to look for one. She shook her fist at all five of them and then went running into the house.

I sat down on the steps for a minute, but Ma came back and pulled me up by the arm.

"William, go out in the front and watch for your Pa," she said, shoving me down the steps, "and the minute you see him coming up the street, you run and tell me. The women will be getting here any time now."

I went around the corner of the house and stood by the front gate watching down the street. I did not have to wait long, because the first thing I knew I heard Pa and Handsome talking. They came walking fast.

"What's the matter, son?" Pa asked, looking up at the five goats on the rooftop. "What's gone wrong?"

"Ma says to get the goats down off the house before the women start coming to the meeting," I told him.

"That's easy enough," he said, hurrying around the corner of the house to the backyard. "Come on, Handsome, and get a hustle on."

"Me, Mr. Morris, you're talking to?" Handsome said. Handsome could not walk fast. He always said his arches hurt him when he tried to walk fast. When he did have to hurry, he trotted.

"Hurry up, Handsome," Pa told him. "Stop complaining."

We got to the backyard and Pa studied the goats on the ridge plate for a while before saying anything. He liked the goats just about as much as I did, and that was why he wanted them in town where he could see them every day. When they stayed out in the country on the farm, we did not see them sometimes for as long as a week at a time, because we did not go out there every day.

The goats had stopped walking back and forth on

the roof and were looking down at us to see what we were up to.

"Handsome," Pa said, "go get the ladder and put it up against the porch roof."

Handsome got the ladder and stood it up the way Pa told him to.

"Now, what to do, Mr. Morris?" Handsome asked.

"Go up there and chase them down," Pa said.

Handsome looked up at the big billy goat. He backed away from the ladder.

"I'm a little scared to go up there where that big billy goat is, Mr. Morris," he said. "He's got the meanest-looking set of horns I ever looked at in all my life. If it's all the same to you, Mr. Morris, I just don't feel like going up there. My arches has been hurting all day. I don't feel good at all."

"Stop that talking back to me, Handsome," Pa said, "and go on up there like I told you. There's nothing wrong with your arches today, or any day."

Just then Ma came out, pinning the white starched collar on her dress that she wore when she dressed up for company. She came as far as the steps and stood looking down at Pa and me.

"Now, Martha," Pa said, talking fast, "don't you

42

worry yourself one bit. Handsome and me will have those goats down from there in a jiffy."

"You'd better get them down from there in a jiffy," Ma said. "I've never been so mortified in all my life. All these women will be coming here to the circle meeting any minute now. What will people say if they see a lot of goats walking around on the roof of my house?"

"Now, calm yourself, Martha," Pa said. "Handsome is on his way up there now."

Handsome was still backing away from the ladder. Pa walked over to where he was and gave him a shove.

"Hurry up and do like I told you," Pa said, shoving him towards the ladder again.

Handsome fidgeted a lot, killing all the time he could by hitching up his pants and buttoning his shirt, but he finally made a start towards the ladder. He climbed to the top and stepped to the porch roof. Then he started backing down again.

"Handsome Brown," Ma said, running out into the yard where we were, "if you come down that ladder before getting those goats off the roof, I'll never give you another bite to eat as long as I live. You can just make up your mind to go off somewhere else and starve to death, if you don't do what Mr. Morris told you."

"But, Mis' Martha, my arches has started paining me again something awful."

"I've warned you, Handsome Brown," Ma said, tapping her shoe on the ground, "and I mean exactly what I said."

"But, Mis' Martha, I—"

"I've warned you once and for all," Ma said.

Handsome looked up at the goats, then down at Ma again, and after that he climbed up on top of the kitchen roof. When he had got that far, he cut his eyes down at us to see if we were watching him.

Just then Ma heard some of the women coming up the street. We could hear them talking almost a whole block away. Ma shook her finger at Handsome and ran inside to lock the front door so the women could not get into the house. She figured they would sit on the porch if she did that, because otherwise they might just walk on through the house and come out on the back porch and see what was going on.

Pa and me sat down on the woodpile and watched Handsome. Handsome had gone as far as the top of the kitchen roof, and he was sprawled on the ridge plate hugging the shingles. He looked awfully small up there.

"Don't you dare let one of those goats get hurt, or fall off," Pa shouted at him. "And take care that those little kids don't get caught in a stampede and get shoved off to the ground. I'll skin you alive if anything happens to those goats."

"I hear every word you say, Mr. Morris," Handsome shouted down. "I declare, I never saw such a slippery place before. But I'm doing the best I can. Every time I move I'm scared I'm about to fall off on that hard ground. I'm scared to breathe, Mr. Morris."

He waited, killing time, to hear if Pa was going to say anything more. After a while, he found out that Pa was not going to answer him, and he inched himself along the ridge plate towards the main roof. When he got to the top of the pitch, he gave one more look down at the ground. He shut his eyes when he saw it and did not look down at us again.

"Take care those goats don't get hurt," Pa shouted.

"Yes, sir, Mr. Morris," Handsome said, sounding far off. "I'm taking the best care I can."

He got to the edge of the main roof and climbed on it. From there to the top where the ridge plate was looked as far again as Handsome had already climbed. He inched his way up the sloping side until his fingers

45

got a grip on the ridge plate. It was easy enough for him to climb the rest of the way to the top. When he got up there, he threw one leg across and sat astride the ridge plate, hugging it for all he was worth.

The goats had gone down to the far end of the roof, getting out of Handsome's way. In order to chase the goats down, he would have to slide himself along the ridge plate to where they were and make them turn around and come back to the kitchen roof, where they could jump to the porch and woodshed, and finally to the woodpile.

Handsome had got halfway across when it looked as if the billy had taken it into his head to come back of his own accord. When the billy started, all the goats came, the big one in front, the medium-sized ones in the middle, and the little kids behind. Handsome saw them coming, especially the billy, because the billy lowered his head until his horns stuck up in the air like lightning-rods.

"Wait a minute!" Handsome yelled at the big goat. "Wait there a minute, I said!"

The goat kept on towards him. When he got four or five feet from Handsome, he stopped, chewed half a dozen strokes, and looked Handsome in the eye.

46

While Handsome and the billy goat were up there staring each other in the eye, Ma came running out into the yard to see if the goats had been chased off the roof.

Just then the billy gave a lunge, and went flying at Handsome with his head tucked down and hooves flying out behind. Handsome saw the goat coming at him in time to duck, but the trouble was that there was not any place he could go except flatter on his stomach. Handsome dug into the shingles with his fingers and held on for all he was worth.

"Look out, Handsome!" Pa yelled when he saw what was happening.

Pa jumped to his feet and started waving his arms at the goat. None of that did any good, though, because the goat flew into Handsome headlong with all his might. For an instant it was hard to tell what was going to happen, because after the billy had butted Handsome, both of them sort of stopped short, like two boards coming together in mid-air.

"Hold on, Handsome!" Pa yelled up there at him.

The next thing we knew, Handsome was coming down the slope of the roof, backward, on the seat of his pants. He slid about halfway down, and then he

47

started spinning around like a top. We had no more than seen that when he left the roof and was coming down into the yard. The first thing we thought of was where Handsome was going to land. The yard was hard and sandy, and there was not a thing there, such as the woodpile at the other end of the yard, to break his fall. But before we knew what had happened, he missed the yard completely and was out of sight. He had gone through the well cover like a bullet.

"My heavenly day!" Ma screamed. "Handsome's gone!"

She tottered and fell in the yard in a dead faint. Pa stooped to pick her up, but he dropped her after he had raised her part way off the ground, and ran to the well to see what had become of Handsome. Everything had taken place so suddenly that there was no time to think about it then. The boards covering the well had been bashed in as if a big two-hundred-pound rock had landed on them.

Pa and I tore across the yard to the well. When we got there and looked down inside, we could not see a thing at first. It was pitch-black down there. Pa yelled at Handsome, and the echo bounced back like a rubber ball and blasted our ears.

48

"Answer me, Handsome!" Pa shouted some more. "Answer me!"

Ma got up and staggered across the yard to where we were. She had a hard time steadying herself, and she came reeling towards us like Mr. Andy Howard on Saturday night. She was still dizzy from her faint when she reached us.

"Poor Handsome Brown," Ma said, clutching at the well-stand to support herself. "Poor Handsome Brown. He was the best darkey we ever had. Poor Handsome Brown."

Pa was busy unwinding the windlass, because he wanted to get the rope and bucket down into the well as quick as he could.

"Shut up, Martha!" he said out of the corner of his mouth, "don't you see how busy I am trying to get this rope and bucket down in here?"

"Poor innocent Handsome Brown," Ma said, brushing some tears from her eyes and not paying any attention to Pa at all. "I wish I hadn't scolded him so much while he was alive. He was the best darkey we ever had. Poor innocent Handsome Brown."

"Shut your mouth, Martha!" Pa shouted at her. "Can't you see how busy I am at what I'm doing?"

49

By that time Ma had got over her fainting spell, and she was able to stand up without holding onto anything. She leaned over the well-stand and looked down inside.

"Are you down there, Handsome?" Pa shouted into the well.

There was no answer for a while. We leaned over as far as we could and looked down. At first there was not a thing to be seen, but slowly two big, round, white balls started shining down in the bottom. They looked as if they were a mile away. Pretty soon they got brighter and then they looked like two cat eyes on a black night when you turn a flashlight on them.

"Can you breathe all right, Handsome?" Pa shouted down at him.

"I can breathe all right, Mr. Morris," Handsome said, "but my arches pain me something terrible."

"Fiddlesticks," Pa said. "There's nothing wrong with your arches. Can you see all right?"

"I can't see a thing," Handsome said. "I've done gone and got as blind as a bat. I can't see nothing at all."

"That's because you're in the bottom of the well," Pa told him. "Nobody could see down there."

"Is that where I am?" Handsome asked. "Lordy me, Mr. Morris, is that why there's all this water around me? I thought when I come to that I was in the bad place. I sure thought I had been knocked all the way down to there. When is you going to get me out of here, Mr. Morris?"

"Grab hold the bucket on the rope, and I'll have you out of there in no time," Pa told him.

Handsome caught the bucket and shook the rope until Pa leaned over again.

"Mr. Morris, please, sir?" Handsome asked.

"What do you want now?"

"When you get me out of here, you ain't going to make me go back up on that roof again where them goats is, is you?"

"No," Pa told him, turning the windlass. "Them aggravating goats can stay on top of the house until they get hungry enough to come down of their own accord."

We had forgotten all about the goats, we had been so busy worrying about Handsome. Ma turned and looked up on the roof. She shook her fist at them, hard. All of them had crossed to the other end of the roof, the end near the kitchen, and they were standing up there looking down at us.

The billy goat looked Ma straight in the eye, and he stopped chewing as he did it. Ma and the billy acted as if they were trying to see which could stare the other down first.

Just then fifteen or twenty of the women who had come to the circle meeting stuck their heads around the corner of the house and looked at us in the backyard. They had got together when they found the front door locked and decided to come around there and see what was going on. They had been able to see the goats on the roof when they came up the street, and they were curious to see what we were making so much racket about back there.

"My sakes alive, Martha Stroup," one of them said, "what's going on here? Those goats up on top of your house is the funniest sight I ever saw!"

Ma wheeled around and saw the women. She did not say a word, but her hands flew to her face, as though she were trying to hide it, and then she ran into the house through the back door. She slammed it shut and locked it behind her. Pretty soon the women went to the front door, but after they had knocked on it a long

time, they gave up trying to get in, and all of them
started down the street. They kept looking back over
their shoulders at the goats on the roof and laughing
loud enough to be heard all over our part of town.

IV

MY OLD MAN AND THE GRASS WIDOW

IV

MY OLD MAN AND THE GRASS WIDOW

W HEN my old man got up earlier than usual and left the house, he did not say where he was going, and Ma was so busy getting ready to do the washing she did not think to ask him.

Usually when he went off like that, and Ma asked him where he was going, he would say he had to see somebody about something on the other side of town, or that he had a little job to attend to not far off. I don't know what he would have said that morning if Ma hadn't been too busy to ask him.

Anyway, he had got up before anybody else and went straight to the kitchen and cooked his own breakfast. By the time I was up and dressed, he had finished hitching Ida to the cart. He climbed up on the seat and started driving out into the street.

"Can't I go, Pa?" I asked him. I ran down the street

beside the cart, holding on to the sideboard and begging to go along. "Please let me go, Pa!" I said.

"Not now, son," he said, slapping Ida with the reins and whipping her into a trot. "If I need you later, I'll send for you."

They clattered down the street and turned the corner out of sight.

When I got back to the house, Ma was in the kitchen working over the cook-stove. I sat down and waited for something to eat, but I did not say anything about Pa. It made me feel sad to be left behind like that when Pa and Ida were going some place, and I didn't feel like talking, even to Ma. I just sat at the table by the stove and waited.

Ma ate in a hurry and went out into the yard to kindle the fire underneath the washpot.

Early that afternoon one of the neighbors, Mrs. Singer, who lived on the corner below us, came walking into our backyard. I saw her before Ma did, because I had been sitting on the porch steps almost all day waiting for Pa to come back.

Mrs. Singer went over to the bench where Ma was washing. She stood and didn't say anything for a while.

Then all at once she leaned over the tub and asked Ma if she knew where Pa was.

"Most likely sleeping in the shade somewhere," Ma said, not even straightening up from the scrub board. "Unless he's too lazy to move out of the sun."

"I'm in dead earnest, Martha," Mrs. Singer said, coming closer to Ma. "I really am."

Ma turned around and looked at me on the porch.

"Run along into the house, William," she said crossly.

I went up on the porch as far as the kitchen door. I could hear there just as good.

"Now, Martha," Mrs. Singer said, leaning over and putting her hands on the edge of the tub, "I'm not a gossip, and I don't want you to think I'm anything like one. But I thought you would want to hear the truth."

"What is it?" Ma asked.

"Mr. Stroup is out at that Mrs. Weatherbee's this very minute," she said quickly. "And that's not all, either. He's been out there at her house all day long, too. Just him and her!"

"How do you know?" Ma asked, straightening up.

"I passed there and saw him with my own eyes,

Martha," Mrs. Singer said. "I decided right then and there that it was my duty to tell you."

Mrs. Weatherbee was a young grass widow who lived all alone just outside of town. She had been married for only two months when her husband left her one morning and never came back.

"What is Morris Stroup doing out there at that place?" Ma said, raising her voice just as if she were blaming everything on Mrs. Singer.

"That's not for me to say, Martha," she said, backing away from Ma. "But I considered it my Christian duty to warn you."

She left the yard and hurried out of sight around the corner of the house. Ma leaned over and sloshed the water in the tub until a lot of it splashed out. After a minute or two she turned around and started across the yard, drying her hands on her apron as she went.

"William," she said, calling me, "you go inside the house and stay there until I come back. I want to think you are obeying me, William. Do you hear me, William?"

"I hear you, Ma," I said, backing toward the door.

She walked out of the yard in a hurry and went up the street. That was the direction to take to get to

Mrs. Weatherbee's house. She lived about three-fourths of a mile from where we did.

I stood on the back porch out of sight until Ma crossed the street at the next corner, and then I ran around the house and cut across Mr. Joe Hammond's vacant lot toward the creek. I knew a short cut to Mrs. Weatherbee's house, because I had passed by it a lot of times going rabbit hunting with Handsome Brown. Handsome had always said it was a good idea to know short cuts to every place, because there was no telling when one would come in handy just when it was needed the most. I was glad I knew a short cut to Mrs. Weatherbee's, because Ma would have seen me if I had gone behind her.

I ran all the way out there, keeping close to the willows along the creek just like Handsome and I had done every time we went out there looking for rabbits. Just before I got to Mrs. Weatherbee's house I stopped and looked around for Pa. I couldn't see him anywhere about Mrs. Weatherbee's house. I couldn't even see her.

Then I crossed the creek and ran up the lane toward the house, keeping close to the fence that was covered over with honeysuckle vines.

It didn't take long to get as far as the garden, and as soon as I looked around the corner post I saw Ida standing at the garden gate. All she was doing was standing there switching flies with her tail. I think she must have recognized me right away, because she pricked up both ears and held them straight up in the air while she watched me.

I had started crawling around the garden fence when I looked across Mrs. Weatherbee's backyard and saw Ma coming jumping. She was leaping over the cotton rows, headed straight for the backyard.

Just then I heard Mrs. Weatherbee giggle. I looked toward the house, and I didn't even have to get up off my knees to see her and my old man. Mrs. Weatherbee kept it up, giggling as if she were out of her head, just exactly like the girls at school did when they knew a secret about something. At first all I could see was Mrs. Weatherbee's bare legs and feet dangling over the side of the porch. Then I saw my old man standing on the ground tickling her with a chicken feather. Mrs. Weatherbee was lying on her back on the porch, and he was standing there tickling her bare toes for all he was worth. Every once in a while he would sort of leap off the ground when she giggled the loudest. She

62

had taken off her shoes and stockings, because I could see them in a heap on the porch.

Mrs. Weatherbee was not old like the other married women, because she had been going to high school in town when she got married that spring, and she had been a grass widow for only three or four months. She lay there on the porch squirming on her back, kicking her feet over the edge, and screaming and giggling like she was going to die if my old man didn't stop tickling her with the chicken feather. Every once in a while she would laugh as loud as she could, and that made everything funnier than ever, because when she did that my old man would leap up into the air like a kangaroo.

I had forgotten all about Ma, because I was so busy listening to Mrs. Weatherbee and watching my old man, but just then I looked across the yard and saw Ma coming. She made straight for the porch where they were.

Everything happened so fast from then on that it was hard to follow what was taking place. The first thing I knew after that was when Ma grabbed my old man by the hair on his head and slung him backward, clear off his feet. Then she grabbed one of Mrs. Weatherbee's bare feet and bit it as hard as she could.

63

Mrs. Weatherbee let out a scream that must have been heard all the way to Sycamore.

Mrs. Weatherbee sat up then, and Ma grabbed at her, getting a good grip on the neck of her calico dress. It ripped away from her just like a piece of loose wallpaper. Mrs. Weatherbee screamed again when she saw her dress go.

By that time Ma had turned on my old man. He was sitting on the ground, too scared to move an inch.

"What do you mean by this, Morris Stroup!" she yelled at him.

"Why, Martha, I only just came out here to do a good deed for a poor widow woman," he said, looking up at Ma the way he does when he's scared. "Her garden sass needed cultivating, and so I just hitched up Ida and came out here to plow it a little for her."

Ma whirled around and grabbed at Mrs. Weatherbee again. This time the only way she could get a grip on Mrs. Weatherbee was to clutch her by the hair.

"I reckon, Morris Stroup," Ma said, turning her head and looking down at my old man, "that tickling a grass widow's toes with a chicken feather makes the garden sass grow better!"

"Now, Martha," he said, sliding backward on the

64

ground away from her, "I didn't think of it that way at all. I just wanted to do the widow woman a kindly deed when I saw her sass growing weedy."

"Shut up, Morris Stroup!" Ma said. "The next thing you'll be doing will be putting the blame on Ida."

"Now, Martha," my old man said, sliding away some more on the seat of his pants, "that ain't no way to look at things. She's a poor widow woman."

"I'll look at it the way I please," Ma said, stamping her foot. "I have to go out and strip the leaves off milk weeds for enough food to keep body and soul together while you go around the country with a mule and plow cultivating grass widows' gardens. Not to mention tickling their bare toes with chicken feathers, besides. That's a pretty howdy-do!"

My old man opened his mouth as though he wanted to say something, but Ma turned Mrs. Weatherbee loose and grabbed him by his overall straps before he could speak a single word. Then she led him at a fast pace to the garden post where Ida was tied up. She took Ida by the bridle with one hand, still pulling my old man with the other, and started across the cotton field toward home. Ida knew something was wrong, because she trotted to keep up with Ma without being told to.

I raced down the lane to the creek, and hurried home by the short cut. I got there only a minute ahead of them.

When Ma came into our backyard leading Ida and my old man, I couldn't keep from snickering a little at the way both of them looked. Ida looked every bit as sheepish as my old man.

Ma glanced up at me standing on the porch.

"Stop that going-on, William," she said crossly. "Sometimes I think you're just as bad as your Pa."

My old man cut his eyes around and looked up at me. He winked with his right eye and went across the yard to Ida's stall, following Ma as meek as a pup. Just before they went into the shed, my old man stooped down and picked up a chicken feather that one of the hens had shed. While Ma was leading Ida inside, he stuffed the feather into his pocket out of sight.

V

THE TIME MA SPENT THE DAY AT
AUNT BESSIE'S

V

THE TIME MA SPENT THE DAY AT AUNT BESSIE'S

Ma got up early and cooked our breakfast and left it warming on the stove for us. I was awake, but my old man still had his head buried under the covers when she rode off with Uncle Ben to spend the day with Aunt Bessie in the country. As soon as she had left, Pa looked out from under the quilt and asked me if Ma said anything before she got in with Uncle Ben and drove away. I told him she didn't say a word, because she thought both of us were still asleep.

While we were getting dressed, Pa said we would have to try to manage to get along somehow by ourselves the best we could until Ma came back that night. Ma always went out to spend the day with her sister once during the summer, and sometimes twice. She said it was the only real vacation she ever got, and that she would like to go more often if she wasn't afraid of what might happen while she was away.

"There's nothing like keeping batch," Pa said, "even if it's only for one day. It's a real treat sometimes not to have any womenfolk around."

After breakfast my old man went out into the sunshine and stretched. It was already hot that morning, and there wasn't a cloud anywhere in sight.

"This sure is a fine day," he said, turning around and looking at me. "The sun's shining, and we've got the whole wide world before us. It's a pity your Ma can't get the chance to spend the day a lot more often with your Aunt Bessie."

He went over to the fence and leaned against it. I saw him looking out across the garden, watching some sparrows scratching under the cabbages. After a while he picked up a rock and threw it at them.

"Let's go fishing, son," he said, turning around. "This is a fine time to go. Hitch up Ida."

I went out to the stable right away and led Ida out into the yard and began brushing her down with the currycomb. Pa told me to curry her good and then to hitch her to the cart.

"I'll be ready to leave as soon as I get back from the store," he said. "I've got to get me a sack of smoking tobacco."

He went into the henhouse and took a couple of eggs from the nests and put them into his pocket to trade for the tobacco.

"Curry Ida down until she looks spick-and-span, son," he said, starting down the street. "I want Ida to look good on a fine day like this."

"Who's going to dig the bait, Pa?" I asked him.

He stopped and thought a minute, and he said to tell Handsome Brown to dig the worms.

My old man went down the street to the store and I called Handsome. Handsome was smiling all over when he came out where I was currying Ida.

"I sure am glad Mr. Morris said we're going fishing," Handsome said. "I've been itching to go fishing for a good long while."

He got a spade and went behind the stable where the earth was damp in the shade of the chinaberry tree. He started digging for fishing worms right away.

Handsome dug a tomato can full of worms while I was hitching Ida to the cart. We climbed in and sat down to wait for Pa to get back. He wasn't long in coming, but he was hurrying faster than I had seen him walk in a long time. He was almost running.

He came rushing up to the cart and I was about to

hand him the reins when he took Ida by the bridle and led her to a fence post. He tied her up in a hurry.

"What's the matter, Pa?" I asked.

"Never mind about going fishing now," he said. "Fishing can wait. We've got to get busy doing something else right away."

"Why, Pa?" I asked. "Why can't we go fishing?"

"Mr. Morris," Handsome said, standing up in the cart, "I done dug a heaping-big can full of the biggest fishing worms you ever saw. They'll be a big loss if we don't go on down to the creek and use them. They're mighty fine worms, Mr. Morris."

My old man started off toward the backyard waving his hand at us and making motions for us to come along. We climbed out of the cart to see what he was going to do.

When we got to the backyard, I saw Pa get down on his hands and knees and crawl under the porch. I didn't know what he was doing under there, so I crawled under behind him.

"What are you looking for under here, Pa?" I asked him. "What's under the house?"

"Pieces of old iron, son," he said. He began raking the dry, dusty earth with his fingers. In a minute or

72

two he brought up a piece of rusty iron that looked like a wheel from an old sewing machine. "There's any number of pieces of old iron laying around the place, and now's the time to get them together. There's a man downtown buying up all the old scrap iron folks bring him and he pays good money for it, fifty cents a hundred pounds. I can't afford to let a chance like this go by without doing something about it. The man might not ever come back to Sycamore again, and it would be a big loss not to be able to make all this easy money. Let's get busy and pick up all the old pieces of iron we can find."

I turned around and saw Handsome crawling in behind us on his hands and knees. "What we doing here under the house like this, Mr. Morris?" he asked.

"Picking up old scrap iron," Pa said. "Get busy and help out."

"Who wants to waste time picking up old pieces of iron," Handsome said, "right when we's ready to go fishing?"

"Shut up, Handsome," Pa said. "Don't you talk back to me like that. Get busy and do like I said."

Handsome crawled off under the main part of the house mumbling to himself. I could see him stop every

73

once in a while and feel around in the dust for iron, but he didn't look as if he cared whether he found any or not.

"Can we go fishing when we finish picking up the old iron, Pa?" I asked.

"We'll go as soon as we get it all picked up and sold," he said. "If everybody'll pitch in and work hard, we'll finish in no time. We'll still have the better part of the day to fish in before your Ma gets back tonight."

We found three or four pieces of an old cookstove, and an old iron tire from a wagon wheel. We carried everything out into the yard and threw it in a pile beside the fence. After that we found a lot of pieces of old iron in the woodshed, and Handsome found an old washpot under the porch steps. Pa found a heavy iron wheel and dumped it on the pile. We worked away as hard as we could for almost an hour after that, turning over the trash pile, collecting all the old horseshoes Ida had worn out, and looking everywhere we could for things made of iron.

In the middle of the morning Pa stopped and looked at the pile we had collected.

"There ain't near as much old iron around the place as I estimated at the start," he said. "We'll be lucky

74

if all the scrap in that pile weighs two or three hundred pounds. We need about a thousand pounds to bring us some real money. A thousand pounds would bring five dollars when we sold it to the man."

"Maybe it ain't worth the trouble fooling around with, Mr. Morris," Handsome said. "We still got plenty of time to go fishing, though."

"Shut up, Handsome," Pa said. "I've made up my mind to make some money selling the man scrap iron, and I'm going to do it. Now, shut up and look some more."

He sent us around to the front of the house to look again, and while we were gone he walked out the back gate into the alley. Handsome and I had found some old rusty door hinges under the front porch, and we threw them on the pile.

While we were sitting down resting, my old man came staggering through the alley gate carrying a big load of iron. He had the handle from a pump, a couple of sadirons, an ax blade, an iron washpot, and a lot of other things. All the pieces looked a lot newer than the things we had found around our house, and the washpot was still warm from having had a fire under

75

it. He threw the load on the pile and went right back through the alley gate again.

When he came back the next time, he was carrying more than ever. He was weighted down so much that his knees sagged when he walked, and it was all he could do to reach the fence and drop the load on the pile. In the second load he had brought a set of shiny monkey wrenches, a pair of fireplace tongs, and a poker, a heavy iron skillet, and a lot of smaller things.

"I don't see how you can find all them things, Mr. Morris," Handsome said. "I done my best, but I couldn't find nothing like it."

Pa didn't say anything, but he wiped his face with his shirtsleeve.

"What are we going to do now, Pa?" I asked.

"Drive Ida and the cart around here, son," he said. "We'll load up and then I'll drive down and collect the money from the man. I figure we ought to have a thousand pounds or more. That'll bring in a lot of money I hadn't figured on before."

Handsome and I led Ida around to the pile of scrap iron, and all of us pitched in and loaded it into the cart. When we had finished, Pa got a drink from the water bucket and climbed in and picked up the reins.

"Is we still going fishing today, Mr. Morris?" Handsome said.

"I'll be back in no time," Pa said, slapping Ida on the back with the reins. "I'll be back as soon as I get the money from the man."

Handsome and I sat down on the steps and watched Pa drive off. We sat there a long time, and the sun climbed higher and higher. After a while Handsome went inside to look at the clock. The sun was directly overhead by then.

We waited another hour, and then I saw Ida's big ears bobbing up and down over the garden fence. We jumped up and ran out to meet my old man. He slapped Ida with the reins and turned into the yard.

"Is we ready to go fishing now, Mr. Morris?" Handsome said. "If we don't hurry and get to the creek, all the fish will stop biting for the rest of the day."

Pa climbed out, holding a brand-new pair of knee-length rubber boots. He put them on the ground while we looked at them.

"When I collected the four dollars for the scrap iron from the man," Pa said, standing back and looking at the rubber boots, "the first thing I thought of was this pair of boots in Frank Dunn's store. I've sure been

77

needing them for a long time. I don't see how I managed to get along without them up to now."

"What is you going to do with them, Mr. Morris?" Handsome asked.

"Wear them like they was meant to be," Pa said.

"I ain't never seen it get muddy enough around here in this sandy country to need knee-high rubber boots," Handsome said.

"That's because you never took the trouble to notice how damp it gets sometimes when it rains," Pa said.

"Maybe so," Handsome said, "but it always manages to dry up half an hour afterward, and it would take that much time to find them boots and put them on. Looks like to me we could have spent all the wasted time fishing. Mis' Martha's going to be coming back here tonight, and I won't have another chance to go fishing until next year. We sure could have caught a lot of fish while you was wasting the time fooling around with them boots."

"You'd better mind how you talk," Pa said. "Now, I've got half a mind to go off to the creek and leave you behind."

"Please don't do that, Mr. Morris," Handsome said. "I didn't mean that about the boots. They're the handsomest rubber boots I ever saw before in all my life. They're the finest kind of things to have handy when it rains. I wish I owned them, because I'd be mighty proud."

Pa got out and went to the water bucket for another drink. Then he came back and laid his hand on the cart.

"Where's the can of worms, son?" he asked.

I ran and got the worms, and all of us climbed in. Pa picked up the reins and was about to slap Ida on the back when Mrs. Fuller came running in through the alley gate. Mrs. Fuller was a widow who lived down on the next street at the end of the alley and took in boarders for a living. She was about fifty or sixty years old, and was always complaining about something.

"Just a minute there, Morris Stroup!" Mrs. Fuller said, running up to the cart and jerking the reins from Pa's hands.

Pa tried to get out of the cart, but she stood in his way.

"Where's the things you took off my back porch, Morris Stroup?" she said. "There ain't a drop of water in my house, and I can't get none, because you walked off with my pump handle!"

"There must be some sort of mix-up," Pa said. "You

know I'm not the sort of neighbor who'd take a pump handle."

"One of my boarders saw you sneak in my backyard and make off with a lot of my things, including my pump handle, Morris Stroup," she said, shaking her finger at Pa. "You took my sadirons, my tongs and poker, and goodness knows what else. Now, I want them back right away, or I'll call the town marshal!"

Handsome slipped off the cart and backed toward the woodshed. He was just opening the woodshed door when my old man turned around and saw him.

"Come back here, Handsome Brown," Pa said.

Handsome stopped backing away.

"I sure owe you an apology, Mrs. Fuller," Pa said. "All that was the purest kind of accident. I happened to be walking through the alley this morning and I saw some old rusty iron laying on the ground. I thought you was trying to get shed of it, and so I just kicked it along out of the way. I thought I was doing you a favor. I remembered that the boys was cleaning up around our house and in the alley, and that's why your things got mixed up with ours."

"You'd better think about doing yourself a favor," Mrs. Fuller said, "if you don't want to go to jail."

While my old man was calling Handsome, Mrs. Fuller turned around and walked out through the alley gate.

"Handsome," Pa said, "bring me them rubber boots."

Handsome went to the porch and brought the boots.

"Now, let this be a lesson to you," Pa said. "You ought to know better than to pick up just anything you find laying around. It may belong to somebody."

"Me?" Handsome said, shaking all over. "Is you talking to me, Mr. Morris?"

Pa handed him back the rubber boots. Handsome took them, but he let them fall to the ground.

"Take them boots down to Mr. Frank Dunn's store and tell him they didn't fit you," Pa said. "Then ask him to give you your money back."

"Me?" Handsome said, backing off. "You mean me, Mr. Morris?"

Pa nodded.

"Then when you get your money back for the boots," my old man said, "take the money and go over where the man is buying the scrap iron and tell him you've changed your mind and want the pieces back. Hand him the four dollars and then start digging in the pile and pick out all the pieces you sold him. When you get everything picked out, especially the pump handle, load them in the cart and bring them straight home. As soon as you get back you can take Mrs. Fuller the things she wants."

"You don't mean me, do you, Mr. Morris?" Handsome said. "Ain't you kind of mixed up a little? Them rubber boots ain't mine, and I—"

Pa picked up the boots and put them in Handsome's arms.

"You made me feel so ashamed of myself for buying rubber boots when it wouldn't be muddy enough to need them that I gave them to you."

"You did?" Handsome said. "When did you do all that, Mr. Morris?"

"Just a little while ago," Pa said.

"I declare, Mr. Morris," Handsome said, "I ain't never wanted rubber boots in all my life! That's one thing I never thought about!"

Handsome tried to give them to Pa, but my old man shoved them back at Handsome. Handsome stood trembling and trying to say something.

"Stop arguing and do like I tell you," Pa said. "I'd hate to see you go to jail on a fine day like this."

He handed Handsome the reins and pushed him up

into the cart. Then he picked up the boots and threw them inside.

After that he slapped Ida on the back with his hand, and she trotted out of the yard and turned down the street. Handsome went on out of sight holding to the seat with both hands and moaning so loud we could hear him until he got all the way downtown.

My old man walked over to where the can of worms was and looked at it for a while. Then he picked up the can and told me to get the spade. We went around behind the shed where Handsome had dug them that morning and he emptied the can on the ground.

The worms started crawling off in every direction, but my old man got a stick and pushed them down into the hole that Handsome had dug.

"Cover them up good, son," he said. "Help them make themselves feel at home. It's too late to go fishing today, but the next time your Ma goes off to visit your Aunt Bessie, we'll do our best to make the most of it."

I covered up the hole while my old man patted the earth down tight so it would stay damp down where the worms lived until the next time we had a chance to use them.

VI

HANDSOME BROWN AND THE
SHIRT-TAIL WOODPECKERS

VI

HANDSOME BROWN AND THE
SHIRT-TAIL WOODPECKERS

THE shirt-tail woodpeckers had been bothering us
for a long time. There were not so many of them
to begin with, but they raised several nests in the spring,
and by the time the young ones were old enough to
peck on wood they made such a racket early in the
morning that nobody could sleep. The 'peckers lived
in the old dead sycamore tree in our yard, and Ma said
the sensible thing to do was to chop it down. My old
man said he would rather see the Republicans win
every election in the country for the rest of time than
to lose the sycamore. He had been nursing it along
ever since I could remember, pruning back the dead
limbs and daubing paint around the 'pecker holes.
After it had been dead for several years, there was not a
single limb left on it, and the trunk jutted straight into
the air like a telephone pole.

Up near the top of the sycamore was where the

shirt-tail woodpeckers lived. They had pecked at it until they had made more holes than I could count. Handsome Brown said once he had counted them, and he thought there were between forty and fifty. At that time of the year, in early summer, after the young ones had come out of the holes and started pecking, there were always a dozen or more of them around the tree. But early in the morning was the worst time. The 'peckers always got up together at the crack of dawn and started pecking on the dead wood, and my old man said he thought there were about twenty or thirty of them always working from then until six or seven o'clock.

"Mr. Morris," Handsome told Pa, "I could get me a .22 and get shed of them in no time."

"If you shoot one of them woodpeckers," Pa said, "it would be just like you shooting the sheriff of the county. I'd haul off and put you on the chain gang for the rest of your life!"

"Please don't do that to me, Mr. Morris," Handsome said. "That's one thing I won't stand for."

The *rat-tat-tat* in the sycamore got worse and worse all the time. The days were growing longer, and that meant that the 'peckers generally started pecking earlier every morning. My old man said they were coming out and starting to peck at three-thirty.

"If them was my peckerwoods," Handsome said, "I'd chase them off and chop down the tree. Then they couldn't do no more pecking."

"You'd better mind how you talk, Handsome Brown," Pa told him. "If anything ever happens to the littlest one of them woodpeckers, or to my sycamore, you'll wish you'd never seen a shirt-tail woodpecker."

During the day nobody minded the 'peckers much, because they were always busy flying off somewhere to get something to eat, or just resting, and if one of them did peck a little on the sycamore, the rest of them did not join in like they all did early every morning for two hours. My old man said he liked to listen to a lone woodpecker pecking, because it was like having company around all the time. Ma didn't say much, except that she was going to have the sycamore chopped down if my old man didn't do something about the *rat-tat-tat* that woke us up every morning before dawn.

Then one morning a whole hour before daybreak we heard the worst clatter in the sycamore we'd ever heard before. It sounded as if forty or fifty people were banging on the side of the house with claw-hammers.

Ma struck a match and looked at the clock on the mantel, and it was three o'clock. My old man got up and put on his shoes and pants and lit the lantern on the back porch. After that he went across the yard and called Handsome. Handsome always slept in the loft over the woodshed. Pa told him to get dressed and come out in the yard right away.

"Them 'peckers won't let me get a wink of sleep," Pa told Handsome. "You come on around to the sycamore with me and help me quiet them down."

I got up and looked out the window. The sycamore was only about ten feet from the window, and in the lantern light I could see everything that was going on. Handsome came dragging his feet over the ground and yawning.

"Handsome," Pa said, "we've just got to figure out some way to make them 'peckers quiet down."

"How you figure on going about it, Mr. Morris?" Handsome asked, leaning against the tree and yawning some more.

"Hitch yourself up there and maybe that'll stop it," Pa told him.

"What you mean, Mr. Morris? Go up that sycamore?"

"Of course," Pa said. "Shin yourself up there right away. I want to get a lot more sleep before the night's over."

Handsome stood back and peered in the darkness towards the top of the tree. The lantern light shone only halfway up, and nobody could see all the way to where the 'peckers were. We could hear the 'peckers up there rapping on the dead wood, and once in a while some big chips and splinters showered down.

"I don't know as how I can," Handsome said protestingly. "I ain't never learned how to climb a tree that didn't have no limbs at all on it. I'd slip backward a heap faster than I could go forward. There wouldn't be no limbs to clutch to."

"Never mind that," Pa said. "When you get halfway up you can get a toe-hold in the woodpecker holes, and it'll be easier than eating pie."

My old man gave Handsome a shove towards the sycamore. Handsome put his arms around the trunk and measured the bigness of it. He hugged it for a minute, and then he groaned.

"I ain't never tried to do nothing like this before, Mr. Morris," he said, stepping back. "I'm scared."

Handsome looked up at the tree in the darkness. We

could hear the woodpeckers pecking away for all they were worth. They pecked so hard it shook the tree all the way down to the ground, and pretty soon the panes in the window began to rattle.

My old man gave Handsome a hard shove and made him start up the tree. As soon as he got started, he went up out of sight like a squirrel. I couldn't see a thing after that, because as soon as he was out of sight, Pa blew the light out of the lantern. He said he could see better in the dark without a light.

In another minute there wasn't a sound to be heard anywhere. The woodpeckers were as still as dead mice.

"How you making out up there, Handsome?" Pa shouted up at him.

There was no answer at all. Pa and I listened, and all we could hear was a sound like a dog panting.

"What's going on up there, Handsome?" Pa shouted.

A big shower of dead bark thundered down from above, pelting Pa on the head.

"Mr. Morris," Handsome said, "you've got to do something to save me quick!"

"What's the matter?"

"These peckerwoods has all started pecking on me,

just like they do on the tree," he said. "Can't you hear them pecking on me, Mr. Morris?"

"I don't hear a thing in the world," Pa said. "Don't let them get you rattled. Just don't pay them no mind. Hang on and try to quiet them down. They ain't making nowhere near as much noise as they were before you went up there."

"That's because they're pecking on me, instead of on the tree, Mr. Morris," he said. "I can't fight them off, because if I did, I'd lose my grip around this here tree."

"Act like you don't notice them," Pa said, "and they'll quit after a while."

"But they just keep on pecking at the back of my head. It's already so sore it feels like it's going to split wide open."

"That's a lot of foolishness," Pa said. "I've lived a long time, and ain't never heard of a woodpecker pecking on a human being."

Pa started around the corner of the house towards the back porch.

"You've quieted them down real good, Handsome," he said. "Now, just stay there and see that they don't start up that pecking on the tree again."

"Mr. Morris!" Handsome yelled. "Where you going, Mr. Morris! Don't go away and leave me up this tree all by myself with all these peckerwoods!"

Pa came on inside, and I could hear him take off his shoes and drop them beside the bed. Handsome started moaning up in the top of the tree, but after a while he stopped making any sound at all. Pa got into the bed and pulled the covers over his head.

As soon as the sun came up, I got out of bed and went to the window. Handsome was still up at the top of the sycamore, but from the way he was hanging on, it looked as if he might slip and fall any minute. Just then I heard Pa get out of bed and start dressing. I put on my clothes as fast as I could and followed him to the backyard.

When we got there, we could see Handsome hugging the tree with both arms and both legs. He had the big toe of one foot in a woodpecker hole, and he was hanging like a scarecrow.

The funny part of it was that there were woodpeckers all over him. Some of them were roosting on his head and shoulders, and a lot of them were hanging to his arms and legs. It looked as if there were twenty or thirty 'peckers on Handsome.

Just then one of the woodpeckers woke up and made

a loud screech. The screech woke up all the other 'peckers, and they all started pecking on Handsome. It looked as if they had worn themselves out and had gone to sleep and then had waked up and remembered that they had Handsome to peck on. Handsome woke up with a jump.

"Mr. Morris! Mr. Morris!" he yelled. "Where is you, Mr. Morris?" Pa and I walked around to the trunk of the sycamore and looked up at the top. The 'peckers would flutter around Handsome and find a better place on him to peck. He flung one arm around his head, trying to shoo them off. But as soon as they flew off for a minute, they came back again and started in just as hard as ever.

"Come on down to the ground, Handsome," Pa said. "I'm up and awake now."

We could see Handsome looking down at us on the ground. After that he flung an arm at the 'peckers and took his big toe out of the hole. He slid down slowly, trying to beat off the birds at the same time.

When his feet touched the ground, he crumpled up like a half-empty potato sack. Pa caught him and pulled him back to his feet.

"You look all tuckered out, Handsome," Pa said.

95

Handsome looked at Pa and me for a minute, but he didn't say anything. He looked too tired to talk.

Just then Ma came around the corner of the house. The woodpeckers were fluttering around over our heads, acting as if they were trying to get at Handsome some more. Suddenly one of the older woodpeckers, a big cock with a long white shirt-tail, got up enough nerve to come down where we were, and he lit on top of Handsome's head. He started pecking on Handsome for all he was worth. Handsome yelled so hard people all over town must have heard him.

"My sakes alive!" Ma cried out. "Just look at poor Handsome's head!"

We had been so busy watching him slide down the tree that we had paid no attention to the way he looked. His clothes were all pecked to pieces, and his overalls and jumper hung around him in rags. But his head looked the strangest of all.

There were four or five big round spots, like woodpeckers' holes in the sycamore, where every bit of Handsome's hair had been pecked away.

Pa walked around Handsome in a circle, looking at him all over. Then he went up and felt two or three of the bald spots on Handsome's head.

"Why didn't you stay awake and keep those 'peckers off you, Handsome?" Pa said. "It was your own fault for climbing up there and going to sleep like that. It wouldn't have happened if you had attended to your business up the tree like I told you. I didn't send you up there to go to sleep."

"You didn't mention to me that you wanted me to stay awake, too," Handsome said, shaking his head. "All you said was to go up there and keep them peckerwoods from making noise, Mr. Morris."

My old man turned around and looked at Ma. They didn't say anything to each other, and in a little while she went around the corner of the house towards the kitchen. We followed, but Ma didn't say anything. She just put our plates down in front of us and helped me to grits and sausage.

97

VII

MY OLD MAN AND THE GYPSY QUEEN

VII

MY OLD MAN AND THE GYPSY QUEEN

A THUNDERSTORM that had been threatening all morning came up while we were eating dinner, but it only sprinkled a little after all. As soon as the shower passed over, my old man got his hat and went down the street to the stores. The sun had come out now again, and in a little while it felt as if there had never been a drop of rain.

While I was sitting there waiting, I heard horses and wagons not far off. It sounded as if there were a lot of them, and the thud of their hooves and the creaking of harness leather came closer every minute. I got up and went out to the middle of the street where I could see better. About halfway to the next corner I saw my old man walking up the middle of the street, waving his arms almost every step, and right behind him were five or six two-horse teams pulling wagons with canvas-covered tops. My old man was waving his arms and trotting a little, and looking back over his shoulder every few steps.

When they got in front of our house, Pa stopped and waved his arms at the drivers, and they pulled the teams over to the side and hitched to the fence posts. During all the time they were tieing up the horses, Pa was waving his arms and urging them to hurry. Then the drivers came running behind Pa while he led them around the corner of the house to the backyard. There were a lot of women and kids inside the covered wagons, and they began piling out, too. Soon it looked as if there were about twenty or thirty people coming towards the house. The women were dressed in long bright-colored skirts that touched the ground, and every one of them wore a red, or yellow, or bright green scarf over her head. The men were dressed like anybody else, except that they wore unbuttoned vests without coats. The kids didn't have on much of anything at all. The grown people and the kids were as dark as Indians, and all of them had long black hair.

The men followed Pa around to the backyard, and the women scattered in all directions, some going up on the porch and some hurrying around to the backyard. All the kids, though, dived under the house right

away. Our house, like everybody else's in Sycamore, was
built high off the ground so the air could circulate under
the rooms and cool them off in hot weather.

Two of the women walked through the front door
just as if they lived there. I stooped down and looked
under the house to see what the kids were doing, and
I saw three or four of them hopping around like rabbits
on four feet. Just then the screen door on the front
porch slammed shut, and I looked up and saw one of
the women run down the steps with something tucked
in her arms. She went straight to one of the wagons, put
something inside, and ran back to the house again.

I ran around to the backyard right away. The men
were looking in the woodshed, in the stable, and everywhere else they could. Some of them were turning over
boards and sticks of wood as if they were looking for
something. While I was watching them, Handsome
came leaping out the kitchen door with one of the long-
skirted women behind. He ran straight to the woodshed
and got inside.

"Now, let's just take it calm and easy," Pa said to
one of the men wearing a vest. "I want to make some
swaps as much as anybody, but I can't think what I'm

doing if I'm rushed. Let's just take it easy and talk things over."

Nobody paid any attention to what my old man said, because everyone was busy looking at things and dashing about. One of the men went to the woodshed and stepped inside. Handsome came out as fast as he could.

Just then I heard Ma scream at the top of her voice inside the house. She had been taking a nap, and it sounded as if the women had waked her up out of her sleep and scared her. It wasn't long until Ma came tearing out of the house.

"What's going on, Morris?" Ma said. "Who are all these strange people, anyway? I was sound asleep when I woke up and saw two women I'd never laid eyes on before in all my life. They were taking the sheets off the bed!"

"Now, just be calm, Martha," Pa said. "I'll have things straightened out in no time. I'll fix things right in a jiffy."

"But who on earth are these strange people?" Ma said.

"They're just some gypsies I met downtown who said they wanted to make some swaps with me. I invited them to come up where we could talk things over. There's a lot of odds and ends about the place that have needed swapping for a long time. I'll be glad to get them out of the way."

Two of the women came out of the house and went up to Ma. Ma backed off, but they pinned her in a corner and started talking so fast nobody could understand what they were saying. One of them began to dance up and down and wave her arms. Then one of the men came to the porch and told Ma the women wanted to swap her for her dress. Ma told them she didn't want to swap her dress, but the women didn't pay her any heed at all.

The kids that had been crawling around under the house came out with my baseball bat and a fielder's glove and raced around the corner of the porch towards the wagons. I started after them, but when I got to the corner, I decided I'd better not try to stop them just then. I called Handsome and told him what they had taken, but he said it would be better not to argue with them. Some of the kids were bigger than either of us, anyway.

"Now, wait a minute, folks," Pa said, trying to grab the men by the back of their vests. "Let's quiet down and talk these swaps over. I want to know what I'm going to get for the things I trade you."

"Morris!" Ma yelled. "Get these people away from here! Do you hear me, Morris!"

Pa was so busy trying to calm them down that he didn't hear a word Ma said. He went to the woodshed and brought out an old ax with a broken handle. One of the men took the ax and looked it over carefully. Then he handed it to another man. The other man hurried out to the wagons with it.

"Now, hold on here!" Pa said. "This ain't no way to swap. I don't seem to be getting nothing at all for my end of the deal. That ain't a fair way to swap. No, sir, it ain't!"

Another gypsy picked up an old tin bucket with a hole in the bottom while Pa was talking, and he handed it to another gypsy who carried it out to the wagons. Pa grabbed one of the gypsies by the back of his vest and tried to argue about the ax and the bucket. While he was doing that, another one of them went into the woodshed and carried out our saw-horse. Pa saw our saw-horse going towards the wagons, but it was gone before he could grab it.

"A swap's a swap," my old man said, "but not when

it's as one-sided as this. You folks have been getting your share, but I ain't got a single thing for mine."

One of the gypsies came over and put his hand in his pocket and brought out a jack knife. Pa tried to open it to look at it, but both blades were broken off.

"Now, hold on," Pa said. "I didn't bargain for nothing like this."

The men climbed up in the woodshed loft where Handsome slept at night, and Pa started up behind them, still trying to make them listen to him.

The gypsy women were plaguing Ma until she was almost out of her mind. They had gone inside and had brought out Ma's sewing basket, a hairbrush, and the water pitcher from the washstand. Ma was trying to take the things away from the women, but they wouldn't turn loose. One of the gypsies handed Ma a string of beads, and the others made off with the pitcher, the brush, and the sewing basket.

One of the men climbed down from the loft carrying Handsome's banjo under his arm. Handsome let out a yell and grabbed the banjo before the gypsy could make off with it.

"Morris!" Ma yelled. "Get these people away from

107

here! Do you hear me, Morris! They're going to ran-
sack the whole place!"

One of the gypsy women grabbed Ma's hand and
looked at the palm. She began telling Ma things about
her future, and Ma got so interested in what she was
saying that she didn't yell any more right away. While
the woman was reading Ma's palm, the others went inside the house.

Pa was so rattled by then that he didn't see one of the
men lead Ida out of the stable. The man had put a
halter around Ida's neck, and she followed him just as
though she didn't know a thing was wrong.

"There goes Ida, Pa!" I yelled. "Pa, don't swap off
Ida!"

Ma heard me and she let out a yell.

"Morris Stroup!" she said. "Are you clear out of
your head! Don't you dare let that mule out of this
yard!"

Pa turned around and saw Ida walking off, and he
looked as if he was so distracted he didn't know what to
do. Handsome grabbed the halter line and pulled Ida
away from the gypsy.

"No, sir!" Handsome said. "Ain't nobody going to
take this here mule!"

"Now, you folks just ain't acting fair and square," Pa said. "I'm in a good frame of mind to make trades, as long as it's pure give-and-take, but I ain't going to stand for such one-sided going on. I'm going to have my say-so about what's traded for what."

Handsome led Ida back to the stable and locked the door.

Some of the kids dashed out of the kitchen with biscuits and baked sweet potatoes that had been left over from dinner. Ma saw them, but she was so mad she couldn't say a word. One of the gypsy women put the string of beads around Ma's neck, and the others tried to take off her shoes. Ma kicked like a mule when they tried to make off with her shoes. Handsome yelled at me, and I turned around. The gypsy kids were crawling out from under the porch carrying the steamshovel we built railroads with under the house. But that wasn't all. One of them had all the engines and cars. The first thing I knew Handsome had grabbed the kids and had taken the things away from them. He gave the kids a shove that sent them flying around the corner of the house.

"They sure got mixed up when they thought they

could get away with these," Handsome said, hugging the steamshovel and train in his arms.

Just then another gypsy woman, one that we had never seen before, came walking into the yard. She looked like all the rest of them, except that she had on a long bright red dress and a lot of bracelets on her arms. The other gypsies all fell back when she walked up to Pa, and all the arguing stopped right away.

"Who're you?" Pa asked, looking her up and down.

"I'm the Queen," she said.

The Queen picked up Pa's hand and looked at the palm. Pa backed up against the stable door while she ran her fingers over his hand as if she was trying to find out something.

"You have a good hand," she said. "You have a strong life line. There is a good future ahead of you. You are a lucky man."

Pa laughed a little and looked around to see if anybody else had heard what she said. All the other gypsies were backing away towards the wagons. The women on the porch left, too. They went through the house towards the front door, but Ma followed them to make sure they didn't touch anything else on the way.

While Pa was thinking about what the Queen had

told him, she took him by the arm and led him inside the woodshed. They went in and closed the door.

Handsome went around to the front to make sure the gypsy kids didn't try to come back and take something else from under the house. I could hear Ma walking around inside as if she was looking to see what was and what wasn't missing. I was standing by the bedroom window when Ma leaned out.

"William!" she said. "Go get your Pa this instant! The sheriff is going to hear about this! I'll have those gypsies arrested if it's the last thing I do! I've already missed your Grandpa's picture from over the mantlepiece, and I can't find my best Sunday dress that was hanging in the closet! Goodness knows what else is missing! Go get your Pa this instant! He's got to notify the sheriff before it's too late!"

I went around to the woodshed where the Queen and my old man were, and when I tried to open the door, it was locked. I started to call Pa, but just then I heard him giggle as if he was being tickled. In a minute the Queen began to giggle, too. Both of them were giggling and saying something I couldn't hear. I went back to the window where Ma was.

"Pa's in the woodshed," I said, "but he didn't hear me."

"What's he doing in the woodshed?" Ma asked.

"I don't know," I said. "He and the gypsy woman who said she is the Queen are both in there."

"Then call your Pa out of there this instant," Ma said. "There's no telling what he's up to."

I went back to the woodshed door and listened. I couldn't hear a single sound, but when I tried to open it, it was still locked. I waited a little while and then called my old man.

"Ma wants you right away, Pa," I said. "You'd better come."

"Go away, son," Pa said. "Don't bother me now."

I went back to tell Ma, but when I got to the window she had left. On the way back to the woodshed, I heard Ma come tearing out of the house. She came as far as the back porch.

"Morris Stroup!" she yelled. "You answer me this instant!"

There wasn't a sound anywhere for a long time, and then I heard the lock on the woodshed door rattle. In a minute or two the Queen stepped out. She took a good look at Ma, and then she hurried around the corner of the house towards the teams and wagons. As soon as she got there, all the men whipped up the horses, and the wagons rattled down the street out of sight.

I looked around, and there was my old man peeping through a crack in the woodshed door. Ma saw him, too, and she hurried across the yard and jerked the door open. My old man was standing there with only his underwear on, and he looked like he didn't know what to do.

"Morris!" Ma yelled. "What on earth!"

Pa tried to duck behind the door, but Ma caught him and pulled him back where she could get a good look at him.

"What does this mean?" Ma said. "Answer me, Morris Stroup!"

Pa hemmed and hawed for a while, trying to think of something to say.

"The Queen told me my fortune," he said, cutting his eyes around to see how Ma was acting.

"Fortune, my foot!" Ma said.

Ma turned around.

"William," she said, "go inside the house and pull down all the window shades and shut the doors. I want you to stay there until I call you."

113

"It really wasn't much to get excited about, Martha," Pa said, standing first on one foot and then on the other. "The Queen—"

"Shut up!" Ma said. "Where are your clothes?"

"I reckon she made off with them," Pa said, looking around the shed, "but I got the best of the deal."

Ma turned and motioned me towards the house. I started off, backing as slow as I could.

"While she wasn't noticing," Pa said, "I got hold of this."

He held up a watch in a gold case. It had a long gold chain, and it looked as if it were brand-new.

"A watch like this is worth a lot of money," Pa said. "I figure it's worth a lot more than my old overalls and jumper, and anything else they carried off. That old ax wasn't worth anything, and that old bucket with the hole in the bottom wasn't, either."

Ma took the watch from Pa and looked at it. Then she closed the door and locked it on the outside. After she had gone into the house, I went back to the wood-shed and looked through a crack. My old man was sitting on a pile of wood in his underwear untying a yellow ribbon that had been tied in a hard knot around a big roll of greenbacks.

114

VIII

THE TIME HANDSOME BROWN RAN AWAY

VIII

THE TIME HANDSOME BROWN
RAN AWAY

HANDSOME was in and out of the house all morning, scrubbing the floor and splitting fat-pine lighters and sweeping the yard with the sedge broom, but we didn't miss him until just before dinner time when my old man went out on the back porch to tell him to take two eggs from the hen nests and to go down to Mr. Charlie Thigpen's store and swap them for a sack of smoking tobacco. Pa called him four or five times, but Handsome didn't answer even the last time Pa called. Pa thought he was hiding in the shed, the way he had a habit of doing, so he wouldn't have to come out and do some kind of work, but after looking in all of Handsome's hiding places, Pa said he couldn't be found anywhere. Ma started in right away blaming my old man for being the cause of Handsome's leaving. She said that Handsome would never have gone off if Pa had treated him halfway decent and hadn't always been cheating Handsome out of what rightfully belonged to him just because he was an orphan colored boy and scared to speak up for his rights. My old man, Handsome, and me played marbles sometimes, and Pa was always fudging on Handsome and breaking up the game by taking all his marbles away from him even when we weren't playing for keeps.

"Anything might happen to that poor innocent colored boy when he gets out in the cruel world," Ma said. "If he hadn't been driven to it, he'd have never left the good home I tried to provide for him here."

"Handsome didn't have the right to run off like he done," my old man said. "It oughtn't to matter how much he was provoked and, besides, it ought to be against the law for a darkey just to pick up and go without a by-your-leave. He might have owed me some money."

"What did you do to Handsome this morning that would've made him run off?" Ma asked him.

"Nothing," Pa said. "Anyway, I can't think of nothing out of the ordinary."

"You done something," Ma said, getting angry and moving towards my old man. "Now, you tell me what it was, Morris Stroup!"

118

"Well, Martha," Pa said, "any number of things might have peeved Handsome and made him run off. I declare, I just can't think of everything."

"You stand there and think, Morris Stroup!" she said. "Handsome Brown would never have gone away like this if you hadn't caused it."

"Well, I did sort of borrow his banjo," he said slowly. "I asked him to lend it to me for a while, but he wouldn't do it, so I went up in the loft where he keeps it in the shed and took it down."

"Where's Handsome's banjo now?" she asked.

"That's something I can't say truthfully, Martha," he answered, standing first on one foot and then on the other. "I was walking along the street downtown last night with it under my arm and a strange colored fellow I never saw before in my life asked me how much I'd take for it. I told him a dollar, because I sort of halfway didn't expect him to have a dollar but, sure enough, he had the money right in his pocket, and so I couldn't honestly back out of the deal since I'd come right out and named the price."

"You go find the darkey you sold Handsome's banjo to and get it back," Ma said.

"I couldn't do that," Pa said right away.

119

"Why couldn't you?" she asked him.

"How in the world am I to know what darkey it was I sold it to?" he said. "It was pitch-black on the street, and I couldn't begin to see the darkey's face. I wouldn't know him now from a million other colored people."

Ma was so mad by that time that it was all she could do to keep from picking up the broom and hitting my old man with it. I guess she didn't want me standing around listening to what she was saying to my old man, because she turned around and called me.

"William," she said, "go downtown right away and start asking people if any of them has seen Handsome Brown. He couldn't have been swallowed up in a hole in the ground. Somebody surely has seen him."

"All right, Ma," I told her. "I'll go."

I ran down the street, leaving Ma and my old man standing on the back porch staring at each other, and went as fast as I could to the ice house where Handsome sometimes went on a hot day to cool off on the wet sawdust. When I got there, I asked Mr. Harry Thompson, who owned the ice house, if he had seen Handsome, but Mr. Thompson said he hadn't seen him in two or three days. I was about to leave and go down to the back door of Mrs. Calhoun's fish market where Handsome went sometimes to get one of the mullets that were too small to sell, when one of the Negro boys who sawed ice for Mr. Thompson told me that Handsome had gone up the street about an hour before to where the carnival had put up the show tents that morning. Everybody knew the carnival was coming to town, and that was why my old man had sold Handsome's banjo for a dollar. I had heard him try to borrow fifty cents from Handsome, but Handsome didn't have any money, and Pa had decided right then and there that the only way he could get enough money to go to the carnival was to sell the banjo. Pa had spent the dollar before he got home with it, though.

I ran back home as fast as I could to let Ma know where Handsome was. When I got there, she and my old man were still standing on the back porch arguing. They stopped what they were saying to each other as soon as I opened the gate and ran up the steps.

"Handsome's gone to the carnival!" I told Ma. "He's up there right now!"

Ma thought a minute before she said anything. My old man moved away from her sideways until he was a good distance out of her reach.

"Morris," she said finally, "I'm going to trust you

this one time more. Go up to that carnival and bring Handsome home before anything dreadful happens to him. I'll never be able to make my peace with the Good Lord and die with a clear conscience if anything should happen to that poor innocent darkey."

My old man started down the steps.

"Can I go, too, Pa?" I asked him.

Before he could say anything, Ma spoke up.

"You go along with your father, William," she told me. "I want somebody to keep an eye on him."

"Come on, son," he said, waving at me. "Let's hurry!"

We hurried down the street, across the railroad tracks, and straight to the carnival lot where the weeds were still growing knee-high in some places.

There were dozens of tents strewn all over the lot, and people were already milling around in front of the shows. The tents had large colored pictures painted on big sheets of canvas stretched across the front of them, and every show had a stand where somebody was shouting and selling tickets at the same time. My old man stopped in front of one of the tents that had pictures of naked girls on it.

"Have you got a dime in your pocket to spare, son?"

he whispered to me. "I'll pay it back to you the first chance I get."

I shook my head and told him all I had was the quarter I had been keeping to pay my way into the Wild West show with when the carnival came to town.

"You just lend me the quarter now, son," he said, poking my pants pocket with his finger. "I'll give it back to you in no time at all. You won't even miss it, it'll be that quick."

"But I want to see the Wild West show, Pa!" I told him, putting my hand in my pocket and locking the quarter in my fist. "Can't I keep it for that, Pa? Please let me keep it! I saved for more than two weeks to get this much."

The man who was selling the tickets picked up a long yellow megaphone and shouted through it. My old man got real nervous and started prancing up and down and pulling at my pocket.

"Now, look here, son," he said. "There ain't a bit of sense in me and you arguing over a little thing like a quarter. By the time you want to spend it, I'll have it back for you, and you won't miss it none at all."

"But Ma told us to find Handsome," I said. "We'd better go look for him, anyway. You know Ma. She'll be as mad as all get-out if we don't find him and take him back home."

"Looking for a pesky darkey can wait," he said, getting a good grip on my arm and trying to pull my fist out of my pocket. "I know what I'm talking about, son, when I say you ought to lend me that quarter you've got in your pocket without a bit more argument. Ain't I always lent you a dime, or whatever it was, from time to time, providing I had it, when you asked me for it? Now, it's only fair that you lend me that quarter for a little while."

Music started up inside the tent, and the man selling the tickets shouted again.

"Hurry! Hurry! Hurry!" he said, looking straight at my old man. "The show's about to begin! The unadorned-dancing-girls-of-all-nations are getting ready to perform! Don't miss the show of your lifetime! Don't live to regret it! Step right up and buy your ticket before it's too late! The girls want to dance—don't keep them waiting! Hurry! Hurry! Hurry!"

"See there, son?" my old man said, getting a tight grip on my arm and pulling with all his might. "The show's about to start and I'll miss seeing it if I don't get in there right away!"

He pulled my fist out of my pocket and pried open my fingers. He was a lot stronger than I was, and I couldn't hold on to the quarter any longer. He got it and ran up to the man selling the tickets. As soon as he could get his hand on it he grabbed the ticket and dashed inside the tent. There wasn't anything I could do then, so I just sat down beside one of the tent stakes and waited. The music began getting louder and louder, and I could hear somebody inside the tent beating on drums. After about five minutes, the music suddenly stopped, and somebody threw back the flaps on the tent. A crowd of men came piling outside, and right behind them, the next to the last one to leave, was my old man. He looked a lot calmer than he did when he went in, but he walked straight into an electric light pole before he knew what he was doing.

"Can I have the change from my quarter, Pa?" I asked him, running and catching up. "Can I, Pa?"

"Not now, son," he said, rubbing the side of his face that had hit the pole. "It's perfectly safe right here in my pocket. You might lose it if you carried it."

We walked up between two rows of tents, looking all the time for Handsome. It wasn't until we had got almost to the last one that we saw him.

125

"Well, what in the world is Handsome doing there?" Pa said, stopping and looking at Handsome.

Handsome was standing behind a big sheet of canvas with his head sticking through a round hole. He was about ten or fifteen yards from a bench that had a lot of baseballs piled on it. A man in a red silk shirt was standing beside the bench holding up both hands full of baseballs.

"Three balls for a dime, and a fine smooth-burning cigar if you can hit the darkey!" he said. "Step right up, folks, and try your aim! If the darkey can't dodge 'em, you get a cigar!"

"How'd you get yourself in a jam like that, Handsome?" my old man shouted at him. "What in the world happened?"

"Howdy, Mr. Morris," Handsome said. "Hi, there, Mr. William."

"Hi, Handsome," I said.

"You ain't tied there, is you?" Pa said. "Can't you get away from there?"

"I don't want to get away, Mr. Morris," Handsome said. "I'm working here now."

"How come you picked up and ran off like you did this morning?"

126

"You know good and well why I left, Mr. Morris," Handsome said. "I just got good and tired of always working for nothing, and having my banjo taken away from me like it was. I just got tired of being treated that way, that's all. But I ain't got no hard feelings against you, Mr. Morris."

"You get yourself away from there and go on back home," Pa said. "Things are piling up all over the place, and there ain't a soul to do them. You just can't run off and quit."

"I've done quit, Mr. Morris," Handsome said. "You ask the white man who's selling them baseballs if I ain't."

We went over to where the man in the red silk shirt was standing. He handed out some baseballs, but my old man shook his head.

"I came to take my darkey back home where he belongs," Pa spoke up. "That one back there with his head sticking through the hole."

The man laughed out loud.

"Your darkey?" he said. "What do you mean, your darkey?"

"That's Handsome Brown," Pa said. "He's been with

us ever since he was eleven years old. I've come to take him home."

The man turned around and shouted at Handsome.

"Say, boy! Do you want to go back to work for this man?"

"No, sir!" Handsome said, shaking his head. "I sure don't! I got myself another job now, and I figure on collecting me some pay instead of never getting nothing at all except some old clothes and things like that."

"Shut your mouth, Handsome Brown!" Pa shouted. "What do you mean talking like that after I've treated you so well all this time? You ought to be ashamed of yourself!"

"I can't help that, Mr. Morris," Handsome said. "I'm working for money-pay, now, and I'm going to keep right on doing it."

"And you ain't coming when I tell you?"

"No, sir, I ain't!"

My old man took out the fifteen cents and laid it on the bench.

"How many of them baseballs do I get to throw for fifteen cents?" he asked.

"Being as it's you," the man said, "I'll give you a special price. I'll let you have six for fifteen. But, remember you've got to hit the darkey before he can dodge out of the way. It won't count if you just throw a ball through the hole. His head's got to be in the hole before it counts."

"That don't bother me none," Pa said, getting a good grip on one of the balls. "Just stand back and give me plenty of room."

Handsome's eyes got whiter and whiter while my old man was warming up by swinging his throwing arm around in a circle just like a pitcher getting ready to throw at a batter.

Pa turned loose with a fast one that caught Handsome square in the forehead before he could dodge out of the way. Handsome was so surprised he didn't know what had happened. He sat down on the ground and rubbed his head until the man in the red silk shirt ran back to find out if anything serious had happened to him. Presently Handsome got up, staggering just a little, and stuck his head through the round hole once more.

"That's one cigar for you, mister," the man said. "You must be an old baseball pitcher, judging by your aim."

"I've pitched a little in my time," my old man said, "but my control ain't what it used to be."

"Well, let's see what you can do this time. That first one might have been just pure luck."

"Stand back and give me room," Pa told him.

He gripped the ball, leaned over and spat on his fingers, and began winding up. All at once he turned loose a spit-ball that went so fast I couldn't even see it. Handsome couldn't have seen it either, because he didn't budge an inch. The spit-ball hit him on the left side of the head with a sound like a board striking a bale of cotton. Handsome sank down to the ground with a low moan.

"Look here, mister," the man in the silk shirt said, running back to where Handsome was stretched out on the ground, "I think you'd better quit chunking at this darkey. He'll be killed if this keeps up much longer."

"You sold me six balls," Pa said, "and I've got a right to chunk them. Tell Handsome Brown to stand up there like he's getting paid to do."

The man shook Handsome a little and got him on his feet. Handsome swayed from one side to the other, and then finally he leaned forward and clutched the canvas. His head was squarely in the middle of the hole.

"Stand back!" my old man yelled at the fellow in the red silk shirt.

He wound up and let the ball go so fast that it had hit Handsome again before anybody knew what had happened. Handsome pitched over backward.

"That's enough!" the fellow shouted at us. "You'll kill this darkey! I don't want no dead darkey on my hands!"

"Then let him come on back home where he belongs," Pa said, "and I'll quit chunking at him."

The fellow ran to a water bucket, picked it up, and splashed the whole bucketful in Handsome's face. Handsome twitched and opened his eyes. He looked at all three of us in a queer sort of way.

"Where am I at?" he said.

Nobody said anything right away. We all waited and watched him. Handsome raised himself on one elbow and looked around. Then he put his hand against his head and began feeling the big round bumps the baseballs had made. The bumps were swelling up like pullet eggs.

"I reckon I done the wrong thing, after all, Mr.

Morris," he said, looking up at my old man. "I'd rather go back and work for you and Mis' Martha, like I've always done, than stay here and get beaned with them baseballs all the time like that."

My old man nodded and made a motion for Handsome to get up. The man in the red silk shirt picked up the balls from the ground and went on back to where he kept them piled up on the bench.

All three of us started home, taking a short cut out through the lot behind all the tents. Handsome trotted along just behind my old man, not saying a word, and trying to keep as close to Pa's heels as he could. He raised his hand to his head and felt one of the big round bumps ever so often.

Just before we got to our house, we stopped and Pa looked real hard at Handsome.

"I'm willing to let bygones be bygones, Handsome," he said. "Now, I don't want you to be pestering me about getting that old banjo back."

"But, Mr. Morris," Handsome said, "I just can't get along without a banjo—"

"Quit arguing about one of the bygones, Handsome."

"But, Mr. Morris, if I could only—"

"Bygones is bygones, and that banjo was one of them," my old man said, turning and walking through the gate into our backyard.

IX

MY OLD MAN AND PRETTY SOOKY

IX

MY OLD MAN AND PRETTY SOOKY

M Y old man picked up one morning long before daylight and went off fishing without saying a word to Ma or me about it. He always liked to go off like that early in the morning before Ma was up and about, because he knew she would put her foot down if she found out what he was up to and not let him go. Sometimes he went off and stayed three or four days at a time down on Briar Creek, and the better the fish were biting the longer he stayed. My old man was a fool about fishing.

He would catch a big mess of catfish and pout-mouthed perch and fry them over a litter fire on the creek bank as fast as he could hook them on his line. My old man said there was not a bit of sense in saving them up to bring home, because the womenfolk never had learned to roll a perch in enough cornmeal to suit his taste.

That morning Ma missed him at breakfast time, but

she didn't say a word to me about it and went on acting just as if she didn't know he wasn't there. After
breakfast I went out behind the shed and helped Handsome Brown shuck the corn and pitch down some hay
for Ida. We stayed out there all morning, splitting pine
lighters and talking about all the money we could make
if we sold all the scrap iron we could find.

When the twelve o'clock whistle blew at the lum-
ber mill, Ma came out behind the shed where we were
and asked Handsome if he knew where Pa had gone. I
didn't say a word, because I never did like to tell on my
old man. I knew all about it just the same, because
Handsome had told me about how Pa had tried to get
him to go along that morning.

"Handsome Brown," Ma said, "don't you sit there
and not answer me when I speak to you. Where is Mr.
Morris, Handsome?"

Handsome looked across at me and then down at the
pile of lighters he had been splitting off and on all morning.

"Ain't he around and about, Mis' Martha?" he said
after a little while, cutting his eyes around and looking
up at Ma until the whites looked like dinner plates.

"You know good and well he's not here, Handsome,"

Ma said, stamping her foot. "The idea of you trying to beat around the bush like that! You ought to be ashamed of yourself!"

"Mis' Martha," Handsome said, looking straight at Ma, "I ain't trying to beat no bushes at all."

"Then tell me where Mr. Morris went this morning."

"Maybe he went down to the barber shop, Mis' Martha. I heard him say only a little while ago that he needed a haircut bad."

"Handsome Brown," Ma said, picking up a little twig like she always did when she was tired waiting for what she wanted to know, "I want you to tell me the truth."

"I'm trying as hard as ever I can, Mis' Martha," he said. "Maybe Mr. Morris went to the sawmill. I heard him say a little while ago he wanted some boards to fix up the hen house with."

Ma turned around and walked to the gate and looked towards our back porch. My old man always kept his fishing pole standing in the corner of the porch when he wasn't using it, and Ma knew about it just as well as anybody else.

"Mis' Martha," Handsome said, "Mr. Morris said

he was going off a piece to look at some calves in a pasture somewhere."

Ma turned around in a hurry.

"Why did he take that fishing pole with him then?" she said, looking hard at Handsome.

"Maybe Mr. Morris changed his mind and forgot to mention it to me," he said. "Maybe he figured it wasn't such a good day to look at the calves, after all."

"It's not such a good day to be telling fibs, either, Handsome Brown," she said, going through the gate towards the house.

Handsome jumped up and ran after her as fast as he could.

"Mis' Martha, I was only telling you what Mr. Morris told me to tell you. You know I wouldn't tell you a fib myself, don't you, Mis' Martha? I only said what I did because Mr. Morris told me to say it, and I always try to do what I'm told to do. Sometimes I get a little mixed up when I try to tell the truth in both directions at the same time."

Ma went into the kitchen and shut the door. We could hear her in there rattling the pots and pans for a long time. After a while she opened the door and called me.

"Your dinner's ready, William," she said. "Your Pa's dinner's ready, too, but he doesn't deserve another mouthful to eat as long as he lives."

Just then I happened to look out across the yard, and I almost jumped out of my skin. There was my old man's head sticking up over the backyard fence just enough for his eyes to show. He was standing behind the high board fence and listening for all he was worth. I nudged Handsome in the ribs so he would see my old man before he said something that might get him into trouble with Pa.

Ma caught on that somebody was hiding behind the fence, and she came to the steps and stood on her toes looking. My old man jerked his head down out of sight just then, but Ma had already seen him. Right away she tore out across the yard and pulled open the gate before Pa had a chance to duck around the shed. She grabbed him by his overall straps and dragged him to the porch steps.

"William," she said to me, "go in the house right this instant and shut the doors and pull down all the window shades. And don't you come out until I call you."

I got up and crossed the porch as slow as I could.

Handsome started backing off around the corner of the house, but Ma saw what he was doing and called him back.

"You stay right where you are, Handsome Brown," she said.

My old man looked pretty sheepish standing out there in the yard with Ma having a good grip on his overall straps. He cut his eyes around and looked at me. I wanted to say something to him, but I was afraid of what Ma might do to me.

"Now, Morris Stroup," she said, leading him to the bottom step. "What do you mean by getting a poor innocent colored boy into trouble by making him tell lies for you?"

My old man looked at Handsome, and Handsome looked down at the ground. Nobody said anything for a long time, and I was afraid Ma would make me go inside before I heard what Pa said.

"Why, Martha," he said in a minute, looking up at her, "there must be a mistake. I've never made Handsome tell a falsehood in my whole life. I wouldn't think of making him do that."

"Then why did you tell him to tell me you were going off to look at calves when you took that fishing pole and went fishing?"

My old man looked at Handsome again, and Handsome tried to look off across the garden.

"If that's what Handsome told you, Martha," Pa said, "it's the truth if it's ever been told, because that's exactly what I've been doing. I saw some of the prettiest-looking heifers—"

Ma looked at him real hard, but she did not say anything right away. It was easy to see that she did not believe a word he said.

She looked at my old man in exactly the same way she did when she still had a lot more on her mind to say but was too mad to say it. After that she called me to eat dinner and went into the kitchen. Pa and I washed up in the basin on the shelf and went in and sat down. We ate what Ma gave us without saying a word. When we had finished, my old man went out into the backyard and sat down against the fence to take his midday nap.

Everything was quiet and peaceful for a little while.

I happened to look up and I saw Handsome making signs for me to come out there. I tiptoed across the yard

143

and opened the gate without letting it squeak a single bit.

When I got behind the shed, Handsome whispered something in my ear and pointed towards the chinaberry tree beside the hen house. There was the prettiest calf standing there that I had ever seen in all my life. The calf was about one-third full-grown, with silky orange-colored hair, and her nose was round and glistening. She was standing in the shade of the chinaberry tree switching flies with her tail and chewing on a bunch of fresh-cut timothy. She looked as if she had never been so contented before in her whole life.

My old man was still asleep against the other side of the fence, and we were scared we would wake him up if we talked out loud. Handsome made signs at me with his hands. It was easy to see that he liked the calf just as much as I did. He walked around her several times, patting her on the rump and rubbing her on the nose.

We were still patting the calf and admiring her when I heard somebody knock on our front door. Just then I looked over the fence and saw Ma come out of the kitchen, wiping her hands on her apron, and going towards the front of the house. I ran around the shed and tiptoed up to the front porch to see who was coming to see us.

There was a man standing on the porch wearing overalls and a field-straw hat. Just then Ma opened the screen door and stepped out.

"Howdy, Mrs. Stroup," he said, taking off his hat and holding it behind him. "I'm Jim Wade from down near Briar Creek."

Ma shook hands with him and said something I couldn't hear.

"I came to ask if you or Mr. Stroup have seen anything of a heifer around your house today," he said. "I lost one this morning, and several people told me they saw one coming up this way not long ago."

"I don't know anything about it," Ma said. "There hasn't been a heifer around here to my knowledge. My husband went fishing this morning, and I'm sure he would have mentioned a calf if he had seen one anywhere."

Mr. Wade turned around and looked up the street for a while.

"It's sure a funny thing," he said. "I was certain I'd find her around your place somewhere. A man down at one of the stores said he saw a heifer come up this way just before the lumber-mill whistle blew at twelve o'clock."

Ma shook her head over and over again, saying she hadn't seen a calf around our house the whole day.

"You know, Mrs. Stroup," Mr. Wade said, shaking his head from side to side, "the whole business is peculiar. One of my field hands said somebody walked across my timothy patch this morning and cut a whole armful of timothy and stuffed it inside his shirt. I didn't pay much attention to that at the time, but about mid-morning another one of my field hands said he saw a man walking up the road towards town with a fishing pole over his shoulder and a heifer following just behind. He told me that the man with the fishing pole stopped ever so often and took a bunch of timothy out of his shirt and tied it to the end of the pole. The heifer followed him all the way up the road out of sight. Pretty soon after that I found that one of my heifers was missing from the pasture. And now that's why I say the whole thing is peculiar. I don't know what to make of it. It sure looks funny."

Ma began to look worried, but she did not say anything right away.

"I wouldn't be bothering you like this, Mrs. Stroup,"

146

he said, "if they hadn't told me downtown that they saw a heifer coming up this way. That's why I stopped in to ask if you'd seen one."

Ma shook hands with Mr. Wade and opened the screen door. After she had gone inside, Mr. Wade walked slowly down the steps, looking up the street and down it. Just before he started walking back towards town, he stooped over and looked all around under our house, which was built about three or four feet off the ground and where there was plenty of head-room for the biggest dogs and almost any sized goat. After he had looked a long time, he got up and dusted off his knees and went on down the street.

I ran back to the shed. My old man was up and nowhere within sight. Handsome Brown was sitting on top of the board fence, with his back to the house, and looking at something on the other side. Just then I heard Ma coming through the house, slamming one door after another, and I got through the gate before she could get to the back porch and see me.

I dashed around the shed, and the first thing I saw was my old man standing in the shade of the chinaberry tree and holding a bunch of fresh-cut timothy for the calf to nibble. Handsome was still on top of the fence watching but not saying a word.

"Pretty Sooky," my old man said to the calf, rubbing her neck and patting her back.

Just then Ma came running through the gate. She stopped dead in her tracks when she saw my old man and the calf.

"Pretty Sooky," he said, stroking the calf. "Pretty Sooky."

Ma moaned just then, and everybody turned around and saw her.

"Martha!" my old man said, coming to the side of the shed and looking at Ma. "What on earth is troubling you, Martha? You look sick."

Ma straightened up and stumbled over the ground towards us.

"Morris—" she said weakly, "What on earth, Morris?"

Pa went back to the calf and held the timothy for her to nibble.

"It was a funny thing, Martha," he said. "I was down at Briar Creek fishing early this morning, and I couldn't get a single solitary bite. I decided to come back home and try again some other morning. On the way I crossed a patch of the finest-looking timothy I've seen in a long time, and I pulled a few bunches, just because I admired it so. It wasn't long after that when I was walking along the road and I just happened to turn around and look behind me, and there was a calf following me. It looked like it was lost. I didn't pay much attention to her until I got home, and then I turned around again and looked behind me, and there she was, the very same calf. I was here in the yard behind the shed by that time, and so the natural thing to do was to give her some of the timothy I'd stuffed into my shirt just because I'd admired it so. It sure was a funny thing, wasn't it, Martha?"

Ma came over and looked at the calf. The calf went on eating the timothy and paid no attention to anybody.

"William," Ma said suddenly, turning around and looking at me, "you go inside the house and shut the doors and pull down the window shades. I don't want you to come outside until I call you."

Every time Ma told me to go inside the house like that it meant she was about to give my old man a scolding. I always hated to go away and leave him when Ma had her dander up, but I had to do what she told me to do.

When she had finished talking to me, she turned and looked up at Handsome on top of the fence. Handsome jumped down as fast as he could without being told.

"Handsome, go on off somewhere and stay until I send for you."

Handsome started walking across the garden right away.

"And if anybody says something to you about a calf, I don't want you to open your mouth, Handsome Brown," Ma said. "The first thing you know you'll be telling fibs on your own account, if you don't watch out. You just stay out of people's way until I send for you. Do you hear me, Handsome?"

"Yes'm, Mis' Martha," he said. "I'll do just like you said. I always try to do just exactly what you and Mr. Morris tell me to do."

Handsome went on across the garden, but I stayed behind the fence out of sight.

"Now, Morris Stroup," Ma said, wheeling around towards my old man. "What have you got to say for yourself now? After going off and stealing Jim Wade's young calf, you ought to have had time to cook up some sort of wild tale. The worst part of it was that you even got Handsome Brown, a poor innocent colored boy, mixed up in your thievery by making him tell a fib for you."

"Now, wait a minute, Martha," he said. "Don't jump at conclusions so fast. This calf just naturally followed me home. I couldn't help it if she—"

"You couldn't help it after you'd gone and cut some of Mr. Wade's timothy to entice her with by tieing it on the end of that fishing pole of yours and dangling it in front of her nose every step of the way here."

My old man looked pretty sheepish while he was trying to think of something to say and wondering at the same time how Ma knew so much about how he had cut the timothy and all the rest.

Ma looked at him real hard, but she did not say anything just then. She watched the heifer nibble the bunch of timothy.

"The only thing I can lay it to," my old man said, "is that the calf just naturally likes to be around me. I don't know no other reason why—"

"As soon as the sun goes down this evening, Morris Stroup, you halter that calf and lead it back to Jim Wade's pasture where you stole it from. And if you meet anybody along the way, black or white, get into the bushes out of sight until they pass, because I don't want it ever to be known you stole a calf and brought it home in broad daylight."

My old man turned and looked at the heifer, and the heifer turned her head and looked up at him. She kept on looking at him, chewing all the while.

"She sure is a pretty little trick, ain't she, Martha?" he said, rubbing the calf on her nose and neck. "Pretty Sooky, pretty Sooky."

The heifer turned and looked at Ma. After a minute or two, Ma went over to the heifer and stroked her on the nose. The heifer kept on looking at Ma straight in the eyes, and Ma acted as if she couldn't stop looking at her.

They stood there a long time looking into each other's eyes, and my old man drew another bunch of timothy from his shirt.

"Pretty Sooky," Ma said, taking the timothy from my old man and holding it for the calf to eat. "It does seem like a shame to take her back out there and make her stay in a pasture all the time. She must get awfully cold at night, and on rainy days."

Pa went over and sat down against the chinaberry

tree and watched Ma and the calf. He did not look a bit
worried any more.

"Pretty Sooky," Ma said, stroking her nose and neck.
"Pretty Sooky."

X

HANDSOME BROWN'S DAY OFF

X

HANDSOME BROWN'S DAY OFF

MA went up the street to the next corner after breakfast to talk to Mrs. Howard about the Sycamore Ladies' Improvement Society meeting, and the last thing she said before she left was for Handsome Brown to have the dishes washed and dried and the dishcloths rinsed and hung out to dry in the sun before she got back. It was Handsome's day off, although he had never had a day off, even though he had worked for us ever since he was eleven years old, because something always seemed to happen that kept him from going away somewhere and loafing for a whole day. Handsome always liked to take his time doing the dishes, no matter whether it was just a regular day like all the others, or whether it was really his day off, because he knew every day always turned out in the end to be the same as any other, anyway; and he generally managed to find a good excuse for not doing the dishes any sooner than he had to. That morning after Ma had gone up to Mrs. Howard's, he said he was hungry; he went into the kitchen and cooked himself a skilletful of hog-liver scrapple.

My old man was sprawled on the back porch steps dozing in the sun, just as he did every morning after breakfast when he had the chance, because he said a nap after breakfast always made him feel a lot better for the remainder of the day. Handsome took a long time to eat the scrapple, as he knew he had the dishes to do when he finished, and he was still sitting in a chair hunched over the cook-stove eating out of the skillet when somebody knocked on our front door. Since both Pa and Handsome were busy, I went around to the side of the house to find out who it was.

When I got to the front yard, I saw a strange-looking girl, about eighteen or twenty years old, standing at the door with her face pressed against the screen trying to see inside. She was carrying a square tan bag made like a small suitcase, and she was bare-headed with long brown hair curled on the ends. I knew right away I'd never seen her anywhere before, and I thought she was a stranger trying to find the house of somebody in town she had come to visit. I watched her until she put her hand on the latch and tried to open the screen door.

"Who do you want to see?" I asked her, going as far as the bottom step and stopping.

She turned around as quick as a flash.

"Hello, sonny," she said, coming to the edge of the porch. "Is your father at home?"

"Pa's taking a nap on the back porch," I told her. "I'll go tell him."

"Wait a second!" she said excitedly, running down the steps and grabbing me by the arm. "You show me where he is. That'll be a lot better."

"What do you want to see him about?" I asked, wondering who she was if she really knew my old man. "Are you looking for somebody's house?"

"Never mind, sonny," she smiled. "You take me to him."

We walked around the side of the house and went through the gate into the backyard. Every time the girl took a step a big wave of perfume blew off of her and her stockings began sagging under her knees. My old man was sound asleep with his mouth hanging open and the back of his head resting on the top step. He always sprawled out that way when he was sleeping in the sun, because he said it was the only way he could feel comfortable while he dozed. I could see Handsome standing in the kitchen and looking out at us through the screen door while he ate the scrapple from the skillet.

The girl put down her suitcase, pulled her stockings up under her garters, and tiptoed to where my old man was sprawled over the steps. Then she got down beside him and put both hands over his eyes. I could see Handsome stop eating just when he had raised a spoonful of scrapple halfway to his mouth.

"Guess who!" the girl cried.

My old man jumped sort of sidewise, the way he generally did when Ma woke him up when he wasn't expecting it. He didn't leap clear off the steps though, because almost as soon as he sat up, the girl pushed his head back and kept him from seeing anything at all. I could see his nose flare open and shut like a hound sniffing a coon up a tree when he got a whiff of the perfume.

"Guess who!" she said again, laughing out loud.

"I'll bet it ain't Martha," Pa said, feeling her arms all the way up to her elbows.

"Guess again!" she said, teasing him.

My old man flung her hands away and sat up wild-eyed.

"Well, I'll be dogged!" my old man said. "Who in the world are you?"

The girl got up from the steps, still laughing, and went for her suitcase. While all three of us watched to see what she was going to do, she opened the lid and took out an armful of brand new neckties. She had more ties than a store.

Pa rubbed the sleep out of his eyes and took a good look at the girl while she was bending over the suitcase.

"This would look wonderful on you," she said, picking out a tie made of bright green and yellow cloth. She went over to where he sat and looped it around his neck. "It was made for you!"

"For me?" Pa said, looking up and sniffing the perfume that floated all around her.

"Of course," she said, turning her head sideways and taking a good look at Pa and the tie. "It couldn't suit you better."

"Lady," Pa told her, "I don't know what you're up to, but whatever it is, you're wasting your time at it. I ain't got no more use for a necktie than a pig has with a side-saddle."

"But it's such a beautiful tie," she said, dropping the armful of ties into her suitcase and coming up

161

closer to my old man. "It just suits your complexion."

She sat down close beside him on the step and began tieing a knot in the tie. They sat there beside each other until my old man's face turned red all over. The perfume had drifted all over the place by that time.

"Well, what do you know about that!" Pa said, looking as though he didn't know what he was saying. "Who'd have ever thought a necktie would've suited my complexion!"

"Let's see you in a mirror," she told him, patting the tie against his chest. "When you look at yourself in a mirror, you'll know you can't get along without that tie. Why, it's perfect on you!"

My old man cut his eyes around and glanced up the street towards Mrs. Howard's house on the corner.

"There's a mirror inside," he said, talking in a low voice as though he didn't want anybody else to hear him.

"Come on, then," the girl said, pulling him by the arm.

She picked up her suitcase and went inside with my old man right behind her. After they were inside Handsome came out of the kitchen and we hurried to the far side of the house where we could look through one of the windows.

"What did I tell you?" the girl said. "Didn't I tell you it was a beauty? I'll bet you never had a tie like that in all your life before."

"I reckon you're right, at that," Pa said. "It's sure a beauty, all right. It sort of sets me off, don't it?"

"Of course," she said, standing behind my old man and looking over his shoulder into the mirror. "Here, let me tie a better knot in it for you."

She went around in front of my old man and drew the knot tighter under his chin. Then she just stood there with her hands on his shoulders and smiled up at him. My old man stopped looking at himself in the mirror and looked at her. Handsome began getting fidgety.

"Mis' Martha'll be coming home almost any minute now," he said. "Your Pa ought to take care. There's liable to be a big fuss if Mis' Martha comes home while he's standing in there like that fooling around with that necktie. I wish I had them dishes all done so I could go and take my day off before Mis' Martha gets back."

My old man leaned over and smelled the air over the girl's head and put his arms around her waist.

163

"How much do you get for it?" he asked her.

"Fifty cents," she told him.

Pa shook his head from side to side.

"I ain't got fifty cents to my name," he said sadly.

"Oh, now, come on and loosen up," she said, shaking him hard. "Fifty cents isn't anything at all."

"But I just ain't got it," he told her, getting a tighter grip around her waist. "I just ain't, that's all."

"Don't you know where you can get it?"

"Not exactly."

Handsome groaned.

"I wish your Pa would stop messing around over that old necktie like that," he said. "I just know ain't nothing good's going to come out of it. I feel in my bones that something bad's going to come along, and it looks like I'm always the one who gets in trouble when something like that happens. I declare, I wish my day off had started long before that girl came here with them neckties."

The girl put her arms around my old man's neck and squeezed herself up against him. They stood that way for a long time.

"I think maybe I could get me a half-a-dollar somewheres," my old man told her. "I've just been thinking about it. I feel maybe I can, after all."

"All right," she said, taking her arms down and backing away. "Hurry and get it."

"Will you wait right here till I come back?" he asked.

"Of course. But don't stay away too long."

My old man started backing towards the door.

"You wait right here where you are," he told her. "Don't budge a single inch from this room. I'll be back before you know it."

In barely any time at all he came running out on the back porch.

"Handsome!" he shouted. "Handsome Brown!"

Handsome groaned as if he were getting ready to die.

"What you want with me on my day off, Mr. Morris?" he said, sticking his head around the corner of the house.

"Never mind what I want," Pa told him, hurrying down the steps. "You come on with me like I tell you. Hurry up, now!"

"What we aiming to do, Mr. Morris?" Handsome said. "Mis' Martha told me to be sure and do them dishes in the kitchen before she got back. I can't do nothing else but that when she done told me to do it."

"The dishes can wait," my old man said. "They'll get dirty after we eat off them the next time, anyway." He grabbed Handsome by the sleeve and pulled him towards the street. "Get a hustle on and do like I tell you."

We went down the street with Handsome trotting to keep up. When we got to Mr. Tom Owens' house, we turned into the yard. Mr. Owens was hoeing witch grass out of his garden.

"Tom," Pa shouted over the fence, "I've decided to let Handsome work for you a day like you wanted. He's ready to start in right away!"

He pushed Handsome inside Mr. Owens' garden and made him hurry up between the rows of cabbages and turnips to where Mr. Owens was.

"Give Handsome the hoe, Tom," Pa said, taking it away from Mr. Owens and shoving it at Handsome.

"But, Mr. Morris, ain't you clear forgot about this being my day off?" Handsome said. "I declare, I just naturally don't want to hoe that old witch grass, anyway."

"Shut up, Handsome," Pa said, turning and shaking him hard by the shoulder. "Mind your own business."

166

"But I is minding my own business, Mr. Morris," Handsome said. "Ain't it my business when I have a day off coming to me?"

"You've got a whole lifetime ahead of you to take a day off in," Pa told him. "Now, start grubbing out that witch grass like I told you."

Handsome raised the hoe and let the blade fall on a bunch of witch grass. The growth was so wiry and tough that the hoe blade bounced a foot off the ground when it struck it.

"Now, Tom," Pa said, turning around, "give me the fifty cents."

"I ain't going to pay him till he does a day's work," Mr. Owens said, shaking his head. "Suppose he don't do a half-a-dollar's worth of work? I'd be cheating myself if I went and paid out the money and then found out he wasn't worth it."

"You don't have to worry about that part of it," Pa said. "I'll see to it that you get your money's worth out of Handsome. I'll be back here ever so often just to stand over him and see to it that he's doing the work like he ought to for the pay he's getting."

"Mr. Morris, please, sir?" Handsome said, looking at Pa.

"What is it, Handsome?" he asked.

"I don't want to have to hoe this old witch grass, please, sir. I want my day off."

Pa gave Handsome a hard look and pointed at the hoe with his foot.

"Now, just give me the fifty cents, Tom," he said.

"What makes you in such a big hurry to collect the pay before the work's done?"

"I've got something that has got to be settled right away. Now, if you'll just hand me the money, Tom—"

Mr. Owens watched Handsome hitting the witch grass with the blade for a while, and then he put his hand into his overalls pocket and took out a handful of nails, screws, and small change. He hunted through the pile until he had picked out half-a-dollar in nickels and dimes.

"This'll be the last time I'll ever hire that colored boy to do anything for me if he don't do a good hard day's work," he told Pa.

"You won't regret hiring Handsome," Pa said. "Handsome Brown's one of the hardest workers I ever seen anywhere."

Mr. Owens handed Pa the money and put the rest

168

of the pile back into his pocket. As soon as my old man had the money, he started for the gate.

"Mr. Morris, please, sir?" Handsome said.

"What do you want now, Handsome?" Pa shouted back at him. "Don't you see how busy I am?"

"Could I get off sort of early this afternoon and have a little bit of my day off?"

"No!" Pa shouted back. "I don't want to hear no more talk about taking a day off, anyway. You don't never see me taking a day off, do you?"

My old man was in such a hurry by that time that he didn't wait to say anything more even to Mr. Owens. He hurried back up the street and ran into the house. He latched the screen door on the way in.

The girl was sitting on the bed folding neckties one by one and laying them in her suitcase. She looked up when Pa ran into the room.

"Here's the money, just like I said!" he told her. He sat down on the bed beside her and dropped the nickels and dimes into her hand. "It didn't take me no time at all to collect it."

The girl put the money in her purse, folded some more ties, and pulled her stockings up around her knees.

"Here's your tie," she said, picking the bright green

169

and yellow one up from the bed and putting it into Pa's hand. The tie fell on the floor at his feet.

"But, ain't you going—" he said, surprised, looking at her hard.

"Ain't I going to do what?" she said right back.

My old man stared at her with his mouth hanging open. She bent over and folded the rest of the ties and put them into the suitcase.

"Well, I thought maybe you'd put it around my neck and tie it again like you did just a little while ago," he said slowly.

"Listen," she said. "I made the sale, didn't I? What else do you want for fifty cents? I've got this whole town to cover between now and night. How many sales do you think I'd make if I spent all my time tieing neckties around people's necks after I'd already made me a sale?"

"But—but—I thought—" my old man stammered.

"You thought what?"

"Well, I kind of thought maybe you'd— I thought maybe you'd want to tie it around my neck again—"

"Oh, yeah?" she laughed.

She got up and slammed the cover on her suitcase. My old man sat where he was, watching her while she picked it up and walked out of the room. The front door slammed and we could hear her running down the steps. In no time at all she was all the way down the street in front of Mr. Owens' house and was turning into his yard.

My old man sat on the bed for a long time looking at the green and yellow necktie on the floor. After a while he stood up and kicked it with all his might across the room, and then he went out on the back porch and sat down on the steps where he could stretch out in the sun again.

XI

MY OLD MAN'S
POLITICAL APPOINTMENT

XI

MY OLD MAN'S
POLITICAL APPOINTMENT

W E were sitting on our front porch after supper when Ben Simons came up the street and turned into our yard. My old man had been feeling bad all evening and hadn't said much out loud, although I could hear him mumbling to himself from time to time. All the trouble had started that morning when Ma jumped on him for not having a job of any kind, and for not even going out to look for one. She had scolded him from one end of the backyard to the other, complaining because she had to take in washing and ironing all the time and because he seldom ever earned any money. Ma's scolding had got under my old man's skin after a while, and he told her if that was the way she felt about it, he would go out and make some money and show her just what he could do when he was pushed. Right away he sent Handsome and me out to get orders for blackberries. He told us to get as many orders as we could and to come back and tell him how many gallons all the orders added up to. Handsome and I spent the whole afternoon going all over town from one house to the next asking people if they wanted to buy some fresh blackberries. Most of them did, because the price was cheap, considering the fact that my old man had told us to tell people that the berries would be clean and that there wouldn't be any ants crawling around among them. He had figured out in his head that if he could sell twenty-five gallons of berries at twenty-five cents a gallon he would make a little over six dollars. He said that was a lot of money for anybody to earn in just one day, and that when he collected it and showed it to Ma, she would be so surprised she would take back all the mean things she had said in the backyard that morning. Handsome and I had finally got orders for twenty gallons, provided they were delivered by supper time the next day. Pa was a little disappointed when we came back and told him we had got orders for only twenty gallons, because he said that meant he would earn a measly five dollars instead of more than six, which he had been counting on. However, he said that was still a lot of money for a day's work, and he told Handsome and me to go out

176

to the country bright and early the next morning and start picking. When Ma heard about it, she came right out and put her foot down hard. She told my old man she wasn't going to let Handsome and me break our backs picking berries for him to sell, and that, besides, it would take us nearly a week to pick twenty gallons. Pa accused Ma of hampering him, and all through supper that night they didn't say a single word to each other. When we went out on the front porch, my old man started in mumbling to himself. He was still doing it when Ben Simons, the town marshal, came into the yard.

"Good evening, folks," Ben said, coming up the steps.

"Howdy, Ben," Pa said. "Come on in and set."

Ma didn't say anything right away, because she was always suspicious of politicians like Ben Simons until she found out what it was they wanted.

"Nice cool evening, ain't it, Mrs. Stroup?" Ben said, feeling in the dark for a chair.

"I reckon," Ma said.

Nobody said anything for a while. Ben cleared his throat several times, sounding as if he wanted to say something but was halfway afraid to open his mouth.

"Busy these days, Ben?" Pa asked him.

"I sure am, Morris," he said right away, opening up just as if he had been waiting for somebody to give him a chance to talk. "I declare, it looks like I never have time any more to sit down for a minute's rest. I snatch a little sleep, and I grab a little something to eat, and the rest is all work, work, work, from early morning until late at night. My wife was telling me only the day before yesterday that I was going to put myself in the grave twenty years ahead of time if I didn't stop working so hard. I have to patrol the streets, keep the jail cleaned up, make arrests, keep my eyes open for bail-jumpers, and the lord only knows what else. I'm worn to a frazzle, Morris."

"Maybe you need somebody to help you out," my old man said. "Now, take me for example. I've got a little free time now and then. True, it ain't much, be-cause I'm kept pretty busy just watching out for my own affairs, but I could spare a little time every once in a while, if it would help you out any."

Ben leaned forward in his chair.

"To tell the truth, that's what I came up here tonight to see you about, Morris," he said. "I'm glad you men-tioned it."

"Ben Simons," Ma spoke up, "I don't know what you're up to, but whatever it is, it had better not be anything shady like the last trouble you got Morris into. I don't want to hear of any more of your money-making schemes like selling family-sized expanding coffins. Nobody in his right mind would want to have a coffin opened up and expanded every time another member of the family died."

"What I had in mind ain't nothing at all like that, Mrs. Stroup," Ben said. "What I'm speaking about now is a political appointment."

"What kind of a political appointment?" she asked, stopping her rocking chair and sitting quiet and straight.

"It's like this," Ben said. "The town council met last night and voted to enforce the ordinance against dogs running loose in the streets. Only two days ago I had to track down and shoot a dog that had gone mad, and the town council thinks it's dangerous to have so many dogs running wild. They told me to enforce the ordinance and lock up every stray dog I found on the street. Right away I told the members that I had all I could handle as it was, and they agreed to appoint an investigator of waifs and strays."

"An investigator of waifs and strays!" Ma said, rising up out of her seat. "Do you mean to sit there, Ben Simons, and say that my husband is the type of man who ought to be a dog-catcher! I've a good mind to ask you to leave my house!"

"Now, wait a minute, Mrs. Stroup," Ben pleaded. "It wasn't my idea at all, in the beginning. One of the council members himself suggested that Morris was the ideal citizen to have the appointment, and they voted—"

"Dogs do have a habit of following me around," my old man said. "I've noticed it all my life. It looks like dogs just naturally take to me—"

"Shut up, Morris!" Ma shouted at him. "I've never heard of such a humiliating thing!"

"But, Mrs. Stroup," Ben said, "a great many famous politicians have started out being dog-catchers. As a matter of fact, most big senators, congressmen, and sheriffs started their political careers as dog-catchers. There's scarcely a high office-holding politician in the country today who didn't begin his career by being a dog-catcher."

"I don't believe it!" Ma said. "I've always had a higher regard for politicians than that."

"Politics is a queer sort of thing," Ben said. "The same rules that apply to other occupations don't seem to hold true to politics. A politician can start out early in his career being a dog-catcher and live it down almost in no time at all. That's what makes politics the kind of occupation it is."

Ma was silent after that, and I could hear her rocker begin squeaking again. It was easy to know that she was thinking hard about what Ben had said.

"The more I think about it," my old man spoke up, "the more I like the idea. I've been thinking for a long time that I ought to take a bigger hand in public life. Just drifting along from day to day, doing a little here and a bit there, don't amount to so much, after all."

"Then you ought to accept this appointment, Morris," Ben said quickly. "It will be a big thing for you. You ought to do it."

My old man sat still and tried to see Ma's face in the dark. She was still rocking back and forth and making the chair squeak as regularly as water dripping from a spigot.

"Well," Pa said slowly, watching Ma as best he could in the dim light, "I reckon it's something I ought to accept." He waited to hear what Ma was going to do.

She paid no attention at all to what he had said. "I'll accept the appointment."

Ben got up.

"That's fine, Morris," he said quickly, moving across the porch towards the steps. "That's fine. I'm glad to hear you say that. I'll expect to see you downtown in the morning right after breakfast."

Ben started down the steps. He reached the bottom one when my old man jumped up and called him.

"Ben," he said anxiously, catching up with him, "how much salary does the office pay?"

"Salary?"

"Sure," Pa said. "How much salary do I get for being the investigator of waifs and strays?"

"Well," Ben said slowly, "it's not exactly a salary."

"What is it then? What do you call it?" '

"It's fees, Morris."

"Fees?"

"Sure, Morris. That's the way most of the best political jobs pay. They pay fees."

"How much fee do I get?" Pa asked him.

"Twenty-five cents for every dog you catch and lock up."

My old man didn't say anything right away. He stood

and looked down the street in the darkness. Ben edged towards the street.

"I reckon I am a little disappointed," Pa said, "because I'd sort of halfway expected to get paid a salary every Saturday night."

"But the thing about fees, Morris, is that there's no limit to how much money you can earn for yourself. When you get paid a salary, you know you'll never get more than a certain amount. But when you get paid in fees, there ain't no limit to your earnings."

"That's right!" my old man said, brightening up. "I just hadn't thought about it that way."

"Well," Ben said, starting down the street, "I'll see you in the morning. Good night."

"Good night, Ben," Pa called after him. "I appreciate you giving me the chance to accept the job."

We went up the steps to the porch. Ma had left and gone inside to bed.

"Let's get a good night's sleep, son," he said to me. "Tomorrow's going to be a big busy day. We'll need all the rest we can get. Come on."

We went inside and undressed and got in bed. My old man tossed and turned for a long time, and I could hear him talking to himself about all the dogs in town he knew by name when I dropped off to sleep.

The next morning as soon as breakfast was over, Pa got his hat and we went downtown to look for Ben Simons. We did not waste any time on the way down the street, but my old man did tell me to remember about Sparky, the coon hound we saw sleeping on Mr. Frank Bean's front porch.

We finally found Ben Simons in the barber shop getting a shave. He had lather all over his face when we first went in, and he couldn't say anything for a while. As soon as he could sit up, though, he waved his hand at Pa and me.

"Good morning, Morris," he said. "All set to start to work?"

"I'm itching to get started, Ben," Pa told him.

"I'll be through here in a minute," Ben said.

After he had got out of the chair and put on his hat he told Pa to go out and round up all the dogs running loose on the streets and lock them up in the big cell-room at the jail.

"Is that all there is to it?" Pa asked.

"It's just as simple as that," Ben told him.

We started off towards the other side of town, walking slow and keeping our eyes open for dogs. Most of them must have been sleeping at that time of the morning, because we didn't see a single one in the streets. After about half an hour, my old man reached in his pocket and took out a dime.

"Here, son," he said, handing it to me, "run down to the butcher shop and get a dime's worth of the biggest piece of meat you can buy for the money. It don't have to be fresh—it just has to be big."

I ran down the street and got a good-sized piece of meat and brought it back to where I had left my old man sitting in the shade of an umbrella tree. He had dropped off to sleep, but he jumped up wide-awake when I shook him and showed him the meat.

"That'll make them take notice!" he said, sniffing at it. "Come on, son!"

We went down another street with my old man swinging the chunk of meat back and forth. It was no time at all before we looked back and saw somebody's speckled bird dog trailing behind us and sniffing the meat.

"That's all that was needed, son," my old man said. "There's nothing like having a good piece of meat at a time like this."

He whistled at the bird dog, and the dog pricked up his ears and trotted a little faster. Pretty soon somebody else's dog got wind of the meat, and he began trotting along behind us. By the time we had reached the railroad crossing, there were seven dogs trailing us. Pa was feeling good about it, and he told me to run ahead to the jail and open the cell-room door. When he got there, he led the dogs inside, and then slipped out with the chunk of meat before they could grab it.

"If we'd got just one more that trip, we'd have made us two dollars," he said. "That's a lot of money to make by just walking up one street and down another one. I'm beginning to see why it is that a political office gets such a hold on a man. I wouldn't want to swap jobs with anybody else in the world now. Being a politician is about the best way to earn a living that I ever heard about."

We went up another street with the chunk of meat, and before we'd gone a block somebody's spaniel came running out from under a house and trotted along behind us. On the way back to the jail I counted five dogs following us. We made a special trip past Mr. Frank Bean's house just to give Sparky a chance to smell the meat and come along with us. After we had locked them all up with the others, my old man sat down and began figuring with a match-stick in the sand.

"That's a little over three dollars, son," he said, throwing the match-stick away. "That's a heap of money to earn in just so little time. Tomorrow if we earn as much, we'll have six dollars. By Saturday night, we'll have eighteen or twenty dollars. That's more money than I thought I'd ever see again in my life. Come on! Let's go home and eat dinner. It's noon already."

We went home and sat down at the table, but Ma didn't say a word, and my old man didn't dare. We finished eating and went outside to sit in the shade of the chinaberry tree.

After about an hour I saw Ben Simons coming up the street in a hurry. My old man was asleep, but I woke him up because I thought Ben had something important to see him about. Ben saw us under the chinaberry tree, and he hurried across the yard.

"Morris," he said blowing hard and all out of breath, "where in the world did you get all them dogs you locked up in the jail?"

"Oh, them," my old man said, raising himself on his elbow. "Why, I just rounded them up like I'm sup-

187

posed to do. It's my job to lock up all the waifs and strays I find loose in the streets. It just happened that these strays were not cows, or horses, or some other kind of animal."

"But you locked up Mayor Foot's prize setter, Morris!" he said excitedly. "Besides that, Mrs. Josie Hendricks said her spaniel was missing, and I found him in the jail with all the others. Mr. Bean's best coon hound was in there with them, too. Every last one of those dogs belongs to somebody, and besides that, the owners paid two dollars dog tax on them. You just can't lock up folks' dogs that they've paid their taxes on!"

"They was running loose on the streets," Pa said. "I went out and made a couple trips looking things over, and I just happened to run across a lot of dogs that acted like they didn't have no homes. It was my duty to lock them up like I done."

"How'd you get them to go in the jail?"

"Well, I sort of led them in, Ben. Dogs always have had a way of following me. I told you that last night."

"You didn't bait them?"

"I wouldn't say that exactly," my old man said. "I did have a little piece of meat, though, come to think of it."

"I thought so," Ben said, taking off his hat and wiping his face with his handkerchief. "I knew something was peculiar."

Nobody said anything for a long time. After a while, Ben put his hat back on his head and looked down at my old man.

"I think maybe I can handle the dog situation from now on, Morris," he said. "Being dog-catcher will probably take up too much of your time."

"But how about the three dollars in fees that I earned?" Pa asked. "I earned them fees, didn't I?"

"I'm not so sure about that," Ben said. "I don't think the town council will want to pay out the money now. Mayor Foot would probably fire me for letting you lock up his prize-winning bird dog if we presented a bill for the fees. One of the first things I learned about politics was that it never was good politics for one politician to step on another politician's toes. I reckon it'll be better if we'll just let matters stand as they are. I can't afford to lose my job on account of you, Morris."

My old man nodded his head and lay back again with his head resting on the trunk of the chinaberry tree.

"I guess you're right about it, Ben," he said. "It looks like being a politician is a full-time job, and I wouldn't want to be saddled with any job that took up all my time, anyway."

XII

THE NIGHT MY OLD MAN CAME HOME

XII

THE NIGHT MY OLD MAN CAME HOME

THE dogs barked at a little before midnight, and Ma got up to look out the window. It was a snowy night about two weeks before Christmas. The wind had died down a little since supper, but not enough to keep it from whistling around the eaves every once in a while. It was just the kind of white winter night when it felt good to be in bed with plenty of covers to keep warm.

The light was burning in the hall, because we always kept one light on all night. Ma did not turn on the light in the room right away. She could see better what was going on outside when the room was dark.

She did not say a word for quite a while. The dogs growled some, and then started in barking again. They were kept chained at the side of the house all night; if they had been allowed to run loose, they would have chewed up a lot of people who came out that way after dark. It was a good thing for my old man, too; they would have chewed him up as quick as they would have somebody they had never smelt before.

"That's him, all right," Ma said, tapping the window-sill with the door key. She was no more mad than usual, but that was enough. When she tapped the woodwork with things like the door key, it was the only sign anybody needed to know how she was feeling.

Presently there was a rumble that sounded like a two-horse wagon crossing a plank bridge. Then a jar shook the house like somebody had taken a sledge hammer and knocked most of the foundation from under it.

That was my old man trying out the front steps and porch in the dark to see if they would hold his weight. He was always afraid somebody was going to set a trap for him when he came home, something like loosening the boards on the porch in such a way that he would fall through and have to lie there until Ma could reach him with the broom or something.

"He's going to come home like this just once too many some of these times," Ma said. "I'm getting sick and tired of it."

"I want to get up and see him," I said. "Please, Ma, let me."

"You stay right where you are, William, and pull

194

those covers up over your head," Ma said, tapping some more on the sill with the door key. "When he gets in here, he's not going to be any fit sight for you to look at."

I got up on my knees and elbows and pulled the covers over my head. When I thought Ma had stopped looking that way, I pulled the covers back just enough so I could see out.

The front door banged open, almost breaking the glass in the top part. My old man never did act like he cared anything about the glass in the door, or about the furniture, or about anything else in the house. He came home once and picked Ma's sewing machine to pieces, and Ma had a dickens of a time saving up enough to get it fixed.

I never knew my old man could make so much racket. It sounded like he was out in the hall jumping up and down to see if he could stomp the floor clear through the ground. All the pictures on the wall shook, and some of them turned cockeyed. Even the big one of Grandma Tucker turned sidewise.

Ma turned the light on and went to the fireplace to kindle the fire. There were lots of embers in the ashes that glowed red when she fanned them with a newspaper and laid some kindling over them. As soon as the kindling began to blaze, she put on two or three chunks of wood and sat down on the hearth with her back to the fire to wait for my old man to come into the room.

He was banging around out in the hall all that time, sounding like he was trying to kick all the chairs down to the far end next to the kitchen. In the middle of it he stopped and said something to somebody he had with him.

Ma got up in a hurry and put her bathrobe on. She looked in the mirror a time or two and straightened her hair. It was a big surprise for him to bring somebody home with him like that.

"You cover up your head and go to sleep like I told you, William," Ma said.

"I want to see him," I begged her.

"Don't argue with me, William," she said, patting her bare foot on the floor. "Go and do like I told you once already."

I pulled the covers up, but slipped them back enough to see out.

The door to the hall opened a couple of inches. I got up on my knees and elbows again so I could see

196

better. Just then my old man kicked the door open with his foot. It flew back against the wall, knocking loose dust that nobody knew was there before.

"What do you want, Morris Stroup?" Ma said, folding her arms and glaring at him. "What do you want this time?"

"Come on in and make yourself comfortably at home," my old man said, turning around and jerking somebody into the room by the arm. "Don't be backward in my own house."

He pulled a girl about half the size of Ma into the room and pushed her around until they were over against Ma's sewing machine. Ma turned on her feet, watching them just like she had been a weathervane following the wind.

It was pretty serious to watch my old man drunk and reeling, and to see Ma so mad she could not get a word out of her mouth.

"Say 'Howdy,' " he told the girl.

She never said a thing.

My old man put his arm around her neck and bent her over. He kept it up, making her bow like that at Ma, and then he got to doing it too, and pretty soon they were keeping time bowing. They did it so much that

Ma's head started bobbing up and down, just like she could not help herself.

I guess I must have snickered out loud, because Ma looked kind of silly for a minute, and then she went and sat down by the fire.

"Who's she?" Ma asked, acting like she was pretty anxious to find out. She even stopped looking cross for a little while. "Who is she, Morris?"

My old man sat down heavy enough to break the bottom out of the chair.

"She?" he said. "She's Lucy. She's my helper nowadays."

He turned around in the chair and looked over at me on my knees and elbows under the covers.

"Howdy, son," he said. "How've you been?"

"Pretty well," I said, squeezing down on my knees and trying to think of something to say so I could show him how glad I was to see him.

"Still growing, ain't you, son?" he said.

"A little, I reckon," I told him.

"That's right. That's the thing to do. Just keep it up, son. Some day you'll be a man before you know it."

"Pa, I—"

Ma picked up a piece of kindling and slung it at

him. It missed him and hit the wall behind him. My old man jumped up on his feet and danced around like it had hit him instead of the wall. He reeled around like that until he lost his footing, and then he slid down the wall and sat on the floor.

He reached over and got his hands on a straight-back chair. He looked it over carefully, and then he started pulling the rungs out. Every time he got one loose, he pitched it into the fireplace.

When all the rungs and legs were out, he started picking the slats out of the back and throwing them into the fire. Ma never said a word. She just sat and looked at him all the time.

"Let's go, Morris," the girl Lucy said. It was the first thing she had said since she got there. Both Ma and me looked at her sort of surprised, and my old man cut his eyes around too, like he had forgotten she was there. "Morris, let's go," she said.

Lucy looked all but scared to death, it was easy to see. Everybody had stared at her so much, and Ma was acting so mad, that it was no wonder.

"Sit down and make yourself comfortable," my old man told her. "Just sit, Lucy."

She reached for one of the chairs and sat down just like he told her to.

The way she was sitting there, and Ma's mad streak on, and my old man picking the chair to pieces was a funny sight to see. I guess I must have snickered again out loud, because Ma turned around at me and shook her finger and motioned for me to pull the covers up over my head, and to go to sleep too, I guess. But I could never go to sleep while all that was going on, and Ma must have known it. I just squeezed down on my elbows and knees as much as I could, and kept on looking.

"When you get that chair picked to pieces, Morris Stroup, you can just hand me over seven dollars to pay for a new one," Ma said, rocking back and forth.

"Shucks, Martha," my old man said. "Shucks, I don't believe there's a chair in the whole world that I'd give more than a dollar, maybe two, for."

Ma jerked out of her spell like a snapped finger. She jumped up and grabbed the broom from the side of the mantlepiece and started for him. She beat him over the head with it until she saw how much damage she was doing to the broomstraw, and then she stopped. She had beat out so much straw that it was scattered all over the floor. After that she turned the broom around and began poking him with the handle.

My old man got up in a hurry and staggered across the room to the closet, throwing what was left of the chair into the fire as he passed it. He opened the closet door and went inside. He did something to the lock, because no matter how hard Ma tried, she could not make the door open after he had closed it.

By that time Ma was so mad she did not know what she was doing. She sat down on the edge of the bed and pinned her hair up a little.

"This is nice goings-on at this time of night, Morris Stroup!" she yelled at him through the door. "What kind of a child can I raise with things like this going on in the house?"

She did not even wait for my old man to answer her. She just spun around toward Lucy, the girl my old man had brought along with him.

"You can have him," Ma said, "but you've got to keep him away from here."

"He told me he wasn't married," Lucy told Ma. "He said he was a single man all the time."

"Single man!" Ma yelled.

She got red in the face again and ran to the fireplace

for the poker. Our poker was about three feet long and made of thick iron. She jabbed it into the crack of the closet and pried with it.

My old man began to yell and kick in the closet. I never heard such a racket as when the dogs started their barking again. People who heard them must have thought robbers were murdering all of us that night.

About then Lucy jumped up, crying.

"Stop that!" she yelled at Ma. "You're hurting him in that closet!"

Ma just turned around, swinging her elbow as she went.

"You leave me be!" Ma told her. "I'll attend to what I'm doing, sister!"

I had to squirm all around to the other side of the bed to keep up with what they were doing at the closet door. I never saw two people carry on so funny before. Both of them were mad, and scared to do much about it. They acted like two young roosters that wanted to fight but did not know how to go about it. They were just flapping around, trying to scare each other.

But Ma was as strong as the next one for her size. All she had to do when she made up her mind was drop the poker, grab Lucy and give her a shove. Lucy sailed across the room and landed up against the sewing machine. She looked scared out of her wits when she found herself there so quick.

Ma picked up the poker again and she pried with all her might and, *bang!* the door sprang open. There was my old man backed up against the closet wall all tangled up in Ma's clothes, and he looked like he had been taken by surprise and caught red-handed with his fist in the grocer's cash drawer. I never saw my old man look so sheepish before in all my life.

As soon as Ma got him out of the closet and into the room she went for Lucy.

"I'm going to put you out of my house," Ma told her, "and put a stop to this running around with my husband. That's one thing I won't stand for!"

She grabbed at Lucy, but Lucy ducked out of reach. Then they came back at each other just exactly like two young roosters that had finally got up enough nerve to start pecking. They jumped around on the floor with their arms flapping like wings and Ma's bathrobe and Lucy's skirt flying around like loose feathers. They hopped around in a circle for so long that it looked like they were riding on a merry-go-round. About that time they got their hands in each other's hair and started pulling. I never heard so much screaming before. My old man's eyes had just about got used to the light again, and he could see them, too, every once in a while. His head kept going around and around, and he missed a lot of it.

Ma and Lucy worked across the room and out the door into the hall. Out there they scuffled some more. While it was going on, my old man stumbled across the room, feeling for another chair. He picked up the first one he could put his hands on. It was Ma's high-back rocker, the one she sat in all the time when she was sewing and just resting.

By that time Ma and Lucy were scuffling out on the front porch. My old man shut the door to the hall and locked it. That door was a thick, heavy one with a spring thumb lock as well as a keyhole lock.

"No use talking, son," he said, sitting down on the bed and pulling off his shoes, "there's nothing else in the world like a couple of females at odds. Sometimes—"

He slung his shoes under the bed and turned out the light. He felt his way around the bed, dragging Ma's high-back rocker with him. I could hear the wood

creak in the chair when he strained on the rungs. He
pulled the covers up, then began picking the chair to
pieces and throwing them toward the fire. Once in a
while one of the pieces hit the mantlepiece; as often as
not one of them struck the wall.

By then Ma and Lucy had got the dogs started again.
They must have been out in the front yard scuffling
by that time, because I could not hear them on the
porch.

"Sometimes, son," my old man said, "sometimes it
appears to me like the good Lord ought never put more
than one woman in the world at a time."

I snuggled down under the covers, hugging my knees
as tight as I could, and hoping he would stay at home
all the time, instead of going off again.

My old man broke the back off the rocker and slung
it in the dark toward the fireplace. It hit the ceiling
first, and then the mantlepiece. He began picking the
seat to pieces next.

It sure felt good being there in the dark with him.

XIII

UNCLE NED'S SHORT STAY

XIII

UNCLE NED'S SHORT STAY

HANDSOME BROWN and I had been down at Mr. Hawkins' water-grinding grist mill almost all afternoon, and about an hour before supper time we started home with the sack of corn meal Mr. Hawkins had ground for us. Ma had sent us down to the mill right after dinner with a bushel of the white field corn Pa kept to feed Ida when Ida was behaving herself and not balking in the middle of the street or kicking the boards off her stall in the barn. While Handsome and I were putting the corn into the sack, Ma had told us to hurry back as soon as the meal was ground because she wanted to make some spoon bread for supper that night. Handsome and I were walking along the short cut through the vacant lot where the carnivals pitched their tents when they came to town and arguing about the baseball game the day before when our town team played the firemen's team from Jessupville over in the next county and which had broken up in the sixth inning when one of the Jessupville firemen hit our town team catcher, Luke Henderson, on the head with a Louisville Slugger bat. Handsome said our town team catcher had scooped up a handful of dust when he thought nobody was looking and had thrown it in the Jessupville batter's eyes just when the pitcher was winding up to throw the ball. I told Handsome a gust of wind had blown the dust and that Luke Henderson, who worked in the Squeeze-A-Nickel grocery store, did not have anything at all to do with it. We were still arguing over it when we started across the railroad tracks. A Coast Line freight train had stopped down at the Sycamore depot but we did not pay much attention to it except just to glance down there to see how many box cars the engine was backing into the siding beside the cotton gin. While we were standing on the track watching the engine and cars, we noticed that somebody was walking at a fast pace towards us. He was leaping over the crossties two at a time.

"We'd better hurry ourselves on home with this corn meal for your Ma," Handsome said, pulling me by the sleeve. "You know what she said about wanting it to make some spoon bread for supper. You'd better obey your Ma."

"Let's wait and see who that is coming up the track in such a hurry," I told him. "He's waving at us to wait for him."

"That's just some old tramp who'll take this sack of meal away from us if we don't hurry and get on home like your Ma told us to do."

Handsome began backing away. He took the sack off his shoulder and hugged it in both arms.

"You'd better listen to me and pay me mind," Handsome said. "I know what I'm talking about. I've seen plenty of them old tramps before and they don't ever do nobody any good. That one coming up here ain't out for no good, I can tell. You'd better come on home like I tell you."

I waited where I was and in another minute the man got to where we were standing. He had been hurrying so fast he was all out of breath, and when he stopped, all he could do was just stand there and pant until his breath came back. He was about as old as Pa, but he moved around faster than my old man ever did, and he looked sort of wild-eyed and nervous. He was wearing a pair of old overalls that had a long rip down the front of one of the legs which looked as if it had been there a long time and that he had not had time to get it sewn up. There was a brand-new brown cap on the side of his head that looked as if it had just come out of a store somewhere. His shoes were all run-down, though, and I could see his little toes sticking through the cracks. The holes were so large that his shoes looked as though each one was made in two pieces. There was a red and yellow bandana tied around his neck the same way brakemen on the Coast Line freights wore them to keep cinders from getting down their necks. He needed a shave worst of all, because his black whiskers were so long and bristly that they stuck out in all directions like the stickers on a cockleburr.

"Son," he said, looking at me real hard, "ain't you Morris Stroup's boy, William?"

"Yes, sir," I answered right away, wondering how he knew what my name was. "Yes, sir, that's me."

"Where's your Pa?" he asked. "Where's he at now?"

"Pa went to the country today to do some work at the farm," I told him. "When he left, he said he wouldn't be home till late tonight."

"I'm your Uncle Ned," he said, reaching out and getting a good hard grip on my shoulder. "Don't you know me, son?"

"No, sir," I said, looking at his black whiskers and

twisting my shoulder to keep his grip from hurting so much.

"The last time I was here, you were just a little squirt," he said, letting me go. "Maybe you were too young to remember your Uncle Ned."

"I reckon I was," I told him.

He turned and looked up the street towards our house.

"How's your Ma these days?" he asked.

"She's pretty well," I said, still trying to remember ever seeing him before. Pa had a lot of brothers scattered all over the country, and I had never seen even half of them. Ma said most of Pa's kin were better off staying where they were and that she did not want any of them coming to visit us. Once I had seen Uncle Stet, who worked on a chain gang off and on, but Ma would not let him come inside our house and after sitting on the front steps for about an hour once he got up and left and I never saw him again after that.

"Who's that shine standing over there?" Uncle Ned asked, nodding his head at Handsome.

"That's Handsome Brown, our yard boy," I told him. "Handsome works around the house when there's anything to do."

213

"I'll bet he ain't never done enough work, all told, to earn a day's board and keep," Uncle Ned said. "Ain't that right, boy?"

"I—I—I—" Handsome said, stuttering like he always did when he was scared. "I—I—"

"See?" Uncle Ned said. "What did I tell you? He ain't even got enough energy to lie about it. All the work that shine's ever done could be counted up and poured into a thimble. Ain't that the truth, boy?"

"I—I—I—" Handsome said, backing away.

"He knows it ain't worth the trouble to lie about," Uncle Ned said, walking off.

He went about a dozen steps and stopped.

"Which way is the house, son?" he asked me.

"Whose house?" I said.

"Why, your Ma and Pa's house, son," he laughed. "You don't reckon I'd come to town like this and not stop in and pay a call on you folks, do you?"

"Maybe I'd better go home first and tell Ma you're coming," I told him. "Ma might not like it if I didn't go and tell her first."

"No," he said right away. "Don't do that. It wouldn't be a surprise if she knew all about it beforehand. The best way to surprise somebody is just to walk in when they ain't expecting you. She might think she'd have to go to a lot of extra trouble if she knew I was coming before I got there."

I started towards home with Uncle Ned right beside me. Handsome stayed behind and did not try to keep up at all. We crossed over the right-of-way and turned up our street. When we got almost there, I stopped and waited for Handsome to catch up with us.

"Handsome," I called to him, "you go on first and give Ma the corn meal. Then after that, you can tell her Uncle Ned's here."

"I'll give Mis' Martha the meal," Handsome said, walking sideways around Uncle Ned, "but I ain't so sure about that other thing you told me. You'd better tell her your own self. Mis' Martha might fly off and put the whole blame on me, and I declare I ain't had nothing at all to do with it. I don't want to get mixed up in trouble when it ain't my fault."

"What you talking about, nigger!" Uncle Ned said, stooping down and picking up a hand-sized rock. "Don't you never talk back like that as long as you live! One more peep out of you like that again, and I'll bash your head in with this rock! You hear me, nigger!"

"I—I—I—" Handsome stuttered.

215

"And quit that stuttering," Uncle Ned said. "If there's one thing in the world I can't stand, it's a stuttering nigger."

Handsome backed away and ran through the gate into the backyard. After he had gone, we walked towards the house and Uncle Ned sat down on the front steps. I didn't know what to do, because I was afraid he would get mad at me the way he had at Handsome if I did anything he didn't like. I stood in the yard in front of the steps and waited.

"How big a farm has your Pa got in the country?" he asked me.

"It covers just one fair-sized hill," I told him. "Pa raised a little corn and some peanuts on it last year, and that's about all. Pa says he doesn't have time to spend on it. Handsome Brown does some plowing on it once in a while, and that's about all."

"Stroups never were much for farming," he said.

We waited to find out what Ma was going to do. During all that time there was no sound at all in the house, but that was because I figured Handsome still had not got around to telling Ma about Uncle Ned.

"It's been a long time since I've seen Morris," he spoke up, "but I don't reckon he's changed much since the last time I saw him. How about your Ma, son? Is she about the same as ever?"

"I reckon so," I told him, listening for her to make some sort of noise when Handsome told her about Uncle Ned.

"To sit here like this in the quiet of the evening you wouldn't think there was a trouble in the whole world," Uncle Ned said out loud to himself. "It sure is peaceful."

I heard a door slam shut somewhere inside the house, and I knew Ma was on her way. I backed down the path away from the steps where Uncle Ned was sitting with his elbows propped up on his knees. In barely any time at all the screen door flew open, and Ma came out on the porch.

"Is that you, Ned Stroup!" she yelled.

Uncle Ned leaped off the steps just as if he had been jabbed with a pitchfork. He landed halfway between me and the porch.

"Now, wait a minute, Martha," he begged, backing towards me and keeping the same distance between himself and Ma. "I just dropped in to pay a brotherly call on you and Morris. You can't blame a man from honoring his blood-kin, now can you?"

"Don't you stand there and try to claim any kin with me, Ned Stroup!" Ma shouted.

"Now, Martha, there ain't no sense in me and you falling out over a little thing like kinship. I'm a changed man. I've had a long time to think things over, and I've decided I wasn't always doing the right thing in life. I turned over a new leaf, Martha."

"You get yourself out of my yard, Ned Stroup. I'm not paying heed to a single thing you say. I'm saddled by law to one Stroup, but there's no power in heaven or earth strong enough to force me to put up with two of you Stroups. I've got my cross to bear as it is, and I'm not going to let it get any heavier."

Uncle Ned hung his head and looked down at the ground. He wiggled one of his little toes through the crack in his shoe and stood there looking at it for a long time. All the time he was wiggling his toe, Ma just stood and glared at him.

"Maybe out of the kindness of your heart you could see fit to give me a bite to eat before you send me on my way," he said slowly, glancing up at Ma from beneath his eyebrows and watching how she took it. "I'm a hungry man, Martha. I ain't had a solitary bite to eat since early yesterday morning. You wouldn't want to refuse anybody a bite to eat just so they could stay alive, would you, Martha?"

"When did you get out of the pen this time?" Ma asked quickly.

"Why, only a few days ago," Uncle Ned said, surprised. "How'd you know I'd been in the pen again, Martha?"

"Where else would anybody in his right mind expect you to be?" she said as quick as that.

Uncle Ned looked down at the ground and wiggled his little toe some more. Ma did not say anything else right away, and all the time she just stood there staring at Uncle Ned. After a while she raised her hand and brushed her eyes when she thought nobody saw what she was doing.

"Come on around to the kitchen door, Ned," she said. "The Good Lord will never be able to say that I didn't lend a helping hand, even though I know it's not the right thing to do. I ought to be calling the town marshal to come and lock you up in the jail."

She went back inside the house, latching the screen door so Uncle Ned could not follow her through the hall. After she had gone, he got up and walked around the corner of the house to the backyard. When we got there, Handsome was sitting on the kitchen steps; but when he saw Uncle Ned coming towards him, he jumped up and ran across the yard and sat down on the woodpile. I went inside while Ma filled a heaping plate of black-eyed peas and sausage. When it was ready, she handed it to me and nodded towards Uncle Ned outside on the steps.

I took the plate out on the porch and handed it to Uncle Ned. He did not say a word, but he looked up at me the same way Pa did sometimes when he wanted to tell me something but didn't want to say it in words. I went over to the corner and sat down while he ate the peas and sausage. Presently Ma called me inside and handed me a cup of coffee to give to Uncle Ned.

After I gave him the coffee he took a long sip from the cup and looked up at me again.

"Son," he said, "always be a good Stroup as long as you live. There's no finer family in the whole world than us Stroups, and we don't want nothing to happen that would make folks think we are a common run of humans like everybody else. Us Stroups haven't got rich like some folks have, and sometimes some of us gets into a little trouble and have to go away for a spell to let things cool off, but taken all in all I don't believe there's a finer family anywhere in the country."

"Yes, sir, Uncle Ned," I said, wondering what Ma would say if she heard.

"I'm a grown man, son, and I know good sound advice when I hear it. That's why I want you to remember what I told you about being a good Stroup. There's not many folks in the world today who can boast of being a Stroup."

"All right, Uncle Ned," I told him. "I'll remember."

Ma came to the kitchen door and looked out. She watched while Uncle Ned scraped the plate clean.

"Did you have enough to eat, Ned?" she asked him, her voice sounding a lot like it did sometimes when she spoke to my old man in front of company. "If you are still hungry, I can fill your plate again."

"That's mighty nice of you, Martha," he said, turning around and gazing at her wistfully, "and I sure do appreciate what you done for me. I'll always think kindly of you, Martha, no matter what happens. You treated me like one Stroup to another."

Just then I looked across the yard and saw Handsome get up from the woodpile in a hurry and back away towards the barn. I was still wondering why he had got up and left in such a hurry when Ben Simons, the town marshal, stepped around the corner of the house with his pistol held out in front of him. He was pointing it straight at Uncle Ned.

"Throw up your hands, Ned Stroup!" Ben shouted. "And don't you dare make a move for your gun. If you do, I swear to God I'll drop you dead in your tracks. I ain't taking no chances with you fellows who are always breaking out of the pen."

Uncle Ned did not say a word while Ben came forward a step at a time and jerked the long-barreled pistol from the belt under his overalls. He kept his hands raised high over his head and made no move to try to get away.

"What does this mean, Ben Simons?" Ma said, coming out on the porch. "What on earth?"

"In case Ned failed to tell you, ma'm," Ben said, "he broke out of the pen three days ago and the warden asked the peace officers in the state to track him down. I figured Ned might be coming here to see his brother and get something to eat and a change of clothes, and sure enough he swung off the afternoon freight about an hour ago. I've been watching him ever since. Now it's time to be going, Ned."

UNCLE NED'S SHORT STAY

Uncle Ned let Ben put the handcuffs on him without a word, and then he stood up. He turned around and looked at me before he started off towards town. "Son," he said, "you just keep on remembering what I said about the Stroups. There's so many of us in the world nowadays that one of us is apt to get out of hand every now and then, but that don't mean that the rest of the Stroups ain't the finest people God ever made. You just go ahead and be a good Stroup like I told you."

"Yes, sir, Uncle Ned," I said, watching him turn and disappear around the corner of the house while Ben Simons kept a tight grip on his arm. "I'll remember what you said."

XIV

MY OLD MAN HASN'T
BEEN THE SAME SINCE

XIV

MY OLD MAN HASN'T
BEEN THE SAME SINCE

WHEN I got up to eat breakfast, my old man was sitting at the kitchen stove, leaning back on two legs of the chair and eating hot biscuits and sorghum molasses for all he was worth. He had put his plate on the apron in front of the firebox as he always did, because he could sit there with the oven door open and reach inside for a hot biscuit without having to get up. My old man was a fool about hot biscuits and sorghum molasses.

He had his mouth full when I went in, and he didn't say anything at first. He looked up at me, though, and winked.

"Howdy, Pa," I said, awfully glad to see him. He had been away for almost a whole week that time.

He didn't say anything until he reached into the oven and got another biscuit. He broke it open, spread butter on it, and laid it on the plate, open. Then he picked up the molasses jug from the floor and poured a good cupful of it on the bread.

"How's your copperosticks, son?" he said, squeezing his fingers around my arm.

"All right," I said.

He felt my muscles.

I sure was glad to see him.

Ma came in then and set my plate at the kitchen table and helped me to bread and molasses and a little bacon. She did not say a word to anybody during the whole time she was fixing my breakfast for me. She stirred around after that, making a lot of noise and racket with the pots and pans. She was as mad as a wet hen.

Pa sat looking across the kitchen, cocking an eye at her every once in a while, waiting for her to say something. Me and him both knew the best thing to do when she was like that was to just wait her out. It only made things worse if we tried to talk to her until she was ready to be talked to. Pa sat in his chair as meek as a tramp asking for a bite to eat.

When I had almost finished eating, she came and stood at the stove, hands on hips, staring Pa down.

"Where have you been this time, Morris Stroup?"

she said, suddenly raising her hand and brushing the hair back from her face.

"Now, Martha," Pa said, ducking his head to one side when he saw her raise her hand, "I haven't been anywhere much."

"Going away from home and staying the-Lord-knows-where four or five days at a time may be your idea of not going anywhere much, but it's not mine. Where have you been?"

"Now, Martha," he said, "I just went down the country a little way."

"Where's that good-for-nothing rooster of yours?" she asked.

"College Boy's out in the chicken pen," he said.

"If I ever get my hands on him," Ma said, stamping her foot, "I'm going to wring his neck off."

Pa's fighting cock, College Boy, was the champion of Merryweather County, Georgia. We had had him for about six months, and when Pa brought him home the first time he said the cock was as smart as people with a college education. That's why Pa named him College Boy. He might have been the champion of the whole nation if Pa could have taken him to all the mains. But Pa didn't have any money to ride on the

229

trains with, and we didn't have an automobile to drive, and the only places Pa could go were the ones he could walk to. That was the reason he had to be away from home so much. It sometimes took him several days to walk where there was going to be a cock fight, because they had to keep changing the places from one part of Merryweather County to another so the sheriff couldn't catch up with Pa and the other men who owned game cocks and pitted them.

Pa hadn't answered Ma, because we knew better than to say anything that would sound as if we were taking up for College Boy. Ma hated the cock worse than sin.

"If you don't think I'm asking too big a favor of you," Ma said, "go down to Mrs. Taylor's and get her washing—if you're not ashamed for people to see you bringing home washing for me to do."

"Now, Martha," he said, "you know that's not a proper thing to say. You know I always like to help out."

She went to the kitchen door and looked out into the backyard to see how the fire was burning under the washpot.

"William," she said, turning around to me, "go out

in the backyard and throw some more pineknots under that washpot."

I got up and started outside to do what she told me to do. When I got as far as the door, she turned on Pa again.

"And when you see Mrs. Taylor, Morris Stroup, you can tell her, and everybody else in Sycamore, how I break my back taking in washing while you go tramping around the country with a good-for-nothing rooster under your arm." She stared Pa down some more. "I'd like to get my fingers around that rooster's neck—and yours, too—just once!"

"Now, Martha—"

"The Lord only knows what would become of us if I didn't take in washing," she said. "You haven't done an honest day's work in ten years."

Pa got up and came out in the yard where I was feeding the fire under the pot. He stood and watched me.

"Son," he said, lowering his voice so Ma couldn't hear, "do you know where you can find a handful of corn somewhere for College Boy?"

He didn't wait for me to answer him, because he knew that I knew what to do. He went out the back gate and down the street towards Mrs. Taylor's house three blocks away. After Ma had gone back into the kitchen, I went to the hen house and got an egg out of a nest and put it into my pocket. I knew exactly what Pa wanted me to do, because he always sent me to Mr. Brown's grocery at the corner when he needed corn for College Boy.

I took the egg to the store and traded it for a poke of corn just like Pa did when I went along with him. Mr. Brown said he had heard that Pa won three dollars at a cocking down near Nortonsville the day before, and he wanted to know why we were trading an egg for the corn instead of paying some of the money Pa had made. I told him I didn't know anything about that, because Pa hadn't said a word about how College Boy did at Nortonsville since he got back. Mr. Brown told me to tell Pa that he wanted a chance to see College Boy in a pit the next time they had one near Sycamore. I went back up the street with the poke of corn in my shirt so Ma wouldn't see it and take it away from me.

Pa was already back from Mrs. Taylor's with the washing, and he had come out behind the chicken house to see if I had brought the corn. The chicken house was about a hundred and fifty feet from the backyard where Ma was washing, and we could stay out there and be out of sight. But we had to keep from talking loud, though, or she could hear us.

Pa was squatting on the ground holding College Boy and wiping him off with a damp rag. College Boy had lost quite a lot of feathers, and he was pretty well tired out. His right leg was sore where the skin had rubbed off when a spur worked loose. Pa said for a while he was afraid College Boy wasn't going to be able to come through, on account of the loose spur, but when he found out he couldn't do any damage with the right one, he went to work with the left one. Pa said it was the closest call College Boy had had since his first pit fight. He said he was going to let College Boy rest until his leg healed up, because he didn't want to run any risks.

Pa wiped him down good, and he let me help him. When he finished with the damp rag, he let me hold College Boy in my arms. It was the first time he had ever let me touch the cock, and I asked Pa if I could go along with him the next time he went to a pit fight. Pa said he wanted me to wait until I was older, but he said it wouldn't be long.

"Your Ma would skin me alive if I took you now,"

233

he said. "There's no telling what she wouldn't do to you and me both."

I held College Boy in my arms and he sat there just as if he never wanted to leave. He was a fine-looking cock with bright red feathers on his neck and wings and dull yellow feathers underneath. His comb folded over on the right side of his head like a cow-lick. I had never known how little he was until then. He wasn't a bit bigger than a medium-sized pullet, but you could tell how strong and quick he was by holding him in your arms. Pa said there wasn't a finer cockalorum in the whole nation.

I handed him back to Pa, and Pa told me to crack the corn. I got a flat piece of iron and a rock and cracked the corn and Pa scooped it up and held it in his hand for College Boy. He ate it as though it were the best thing in the world, and he acted as if he couldn't get enough. He ate up the corn as fast as I could crack it.

All the time we were out behind the chicken house, Ma was in the backyard boiling the washing. She was doing Mrs. Taylor's washing then, but there were six or seven others that she did every week, too. It looked as if she washed every day and ironed all night.

We stayed out there a long time watching College

Boy. He had a dust-bed in one corner of the run, and he liked to lie there in the shade and flap dust under his feathers with his wings.

I told Pa I hoped he wasn't going away again soon, because I wanted him to stay at home and let me help him crack corn and feed College Boy every day. He said he wasn't going anywhere for a while, anyway, because he thought College Boy needed at least a week's rest.

We sat there on the ground in the shade a long time until noon. Then Ma called to us to come and eat. When we had finished, she told Pa she wanted him to carry Mrs. Dolan's washing to her. Mrs. Dolan lived on the other side of town, and it was a long walk over there and back. I asked Ma if I could go along and help carry the washing, and she said I could.

We took the washing right after we finished eating, and I thought we would get back in time to go out and see College Boy again before it was too dark. But it was late when we came through town on our way back, and Pa said he wanted to stop at the post office and talk to some men for a while. We must have stayed there two or three hours, because when we did get home, it was pitch-dark. Ma heard us on the front

porch and she came out and asked Pa for the money
he had collected for Mrs. Dolan's washing. Pa gave her
the fifty cents and asked her how long before supper
would be ready. She said it would be soon, and so we
sat down on the porch.

It felt good to be sitting on the front porch with my
old man, because he was away from home so much I
never had a chance to be with him very often. My old
man lighted a cigar stub he had been saving, and we
sat there and he puffed on it in the dark, and the smoke
drifted across the porch, smelling good in the night
breeze.

"Son," he said after a while, "as soon as you've had
your breakfast in the morning, I want you to go down
to Brown's grocery. Get another egg out of the chicken
house and take it down and swap it for some more corn.
As soon as breakfast is over, I'll want to feed College
Boy. He's pretty well tuckered out, and I want to feed
him well so he'll get his strength back."

"All right, Pa," I told him. "I sure will."

We sat there in the dark thinking about the cock.

Ma called us in a little while and we went inside and
sat down at the supper table. There wasn't much on
the table to eat that night, except a big chicken pie. It

236

was in a big deep pan with a thick brown crust over it, and Pa helped me first, and then Ma. After that he took a big helping for himself.

Ma didn't have much to say, and Pa was scared to talk. He never started in talking much, anyway, until he was sure of his ground. We sat at the table eating the chicken pie and not saying anything much until the pie was all gone. Pa leaned back and looked at me, and it was easy to see that he thought a lot of Ma's cooking.

It was as quiet as the inside of a church after the congregation had left.

"Morris," Ma said, laying her knife and fork in a neat row on her plate, "I hope this will be a lesson to you."

"Hope what will, Martha?" he said.

She looked down at the way she had laid her knife and fork on the plate, moved them just a little, and then looked him straight in the face.

"I hope you'll never bring another game rooster to this house as long as you live," she said. "I had to do something desperate—"

"What?" he said, leaning over the table towards her.

"I made this chicken pie out of the one—"

"College Boy!" Pa said, pushing his chair back a little.

Ma nodded her head.

My old man's face turned white and his hands dropped down beside him. He opened his mouth to say something, but he made no sound. I don't know how long it was, but it seemed as though it were half the night before anybody moved after that.

Ma was the first one to say anything.

"It was a harsh thing to do, Morris," she said, "but something drastic had to be done."

"That was College Boy, Ma," I said, "you shouldn't—"

"Be quiet, William," she said, turning to me.

"You shouldn't have done that, Martha," Pa said, pushing his chair back and getting to his feet. "Not to College Boy, anyway. He was—"

He did not say anything more after that. The next thing he did was to turn around and go through the house to the front porch.

I got up and went through the house behind him. It was darker than ever on the porch and I couldn't see anything at all after being where the light was. I felt on all the chairs for him, but he was not there. The

MY OLD MAN HASN'T BEEN THE SAME SINCE
cigar stub he had left on the porch railing when we
went inside to supper was still burning, and it smelled
just like my old man. I hurried down the steps and ran
down the street trying to catch up with him before it
was too late to find him in the dark.